The Awakening of Meeachan Park

A Speculative Fiction Novella
By Elle Hawkweed

Filidh Publishing

The Awakening of Meeachan Park
A Speculative Fiction Novella
By Elle Hawkweed
Copyright © 2023 Filidh Publishing Corp,
First Printing: June 2023
ISBN 978-1-927848-80-7

Filidh Publishing Corp., Victoria, BC, Canada
https://filidhbooks.com

Danny Weeds and Alex Florin - Cover design
Insjoy - istockphoto ID: 1167933869 (Cover Art)
Drew Holloway - Shutterstock ID: 1232371216 (Cover)
Happy Colours Lab - Shutterstock photo ID: 1764061592 (Author photo)

"You cannot get through a single day without having an impact on the world around you. What you do makes a difference, and you have to decide what kind of difference you want to make."
– Dr. Jane Goodall

Prologue

This is a short novel of speculative urban fiction in that it is set in a future version of Victoria, British Columbia, Canada, and it ponders the question of "what if."

We meet the culturally diverse citizens of the city and surrounding area and share in the beauty of the city's crown jewel – the parkland of Meeachan, currently known as Beacon Hill Park. I have chosen to use the original Indigenous name for the area to honour a delightful movement to return to using Indigenous place names.

The city's management of the park's manicured lawns and various outbuildings is taxed as it continues to be home to many unhoused people. A construction project in the park unearths ancient wisdom, and the novel embraces magical realism as strange things happen, changelings abound, and yet life goes on.

Sometimes, looking to the past is the best way to find hope for the future. Transformative change is complex and can require courage and faith to embrace. Fear can also be an incentive.

Elle Hawkweed
2023

Chapter One

The cab pulled around the cul de sac and stopped by *the red car parked just there* as requested. The interior light came on, and the necessary transaction was accomplished quickly. Peter Primeau unfolded his long frame out of the right rear door and grimaced as his head grazed the door frame. Lisa Atkinson wrangled her legs, skirt, and purse all tangled together and alighted from the left rear door.

Slam. "Thank you! Have a good night!" *Slam*.

Peter stretched and yawned as he walked. It had been a long day. His one knee had been troubling him for a while, and standing all day in the bakery was becoming harder on him every day. He was not a young man anymore, which did not sit well with him. **Not at all**. He liked that no one believed he was old enough to retire, or so the other staff had said. His dark brown mop of hair only displayed a hint of salt and pepper when cropped closely at the temples, and there were some patches of grey in his goatee. He did not look his 66 years,

They made their way from the parking lot, down a few uneven steps to the small walkway and then to their door. It had snowed, and the walk was a bit slick, but Lisa also felt her beverage choices in the crisp air. Peter always held his hand out to help her down the stairs. She always waved him off, but he worried. Lisa had opted for early retirement the year before - as soon after her 60th birthday as possible. He'd been quite envious of her freedom and ability to dive into various projects in her home business while he was still trudging off to the bakery. Unfortunately, she had diabetes and struggled with co-morbidities, and having Covid impacted her greatly. She found that working from home was not conducive to keeping physically active, so she took on some short-term government contracts after about six months. Initially, her body had complained vigorously, but she fairly danced down the stairs tonight. Lisa didn't look much over 45 and worked hard at that.

The snow caressed the shrubs and sleeping flowerpots around the entryway, making it quite pretty in the moonlight. The light over the front door came on as Peter fumbled with his keys.

"Hey, sorry. I forgot to turn on the outside light!" said a tall, greying man as he opened the door.

Peter and Lisa entered the home, and after shoes, jackets and a purse were tucked away, they joined the other man in the living room. The television displayed a commercial for window replacements, and the volume was muted.

"Well, that's done, then," said Karl Lappan. He sat back in his recliner, raising the foot panel and stretching his long legs. He and Peter were well over six feet, overshadowing Lisa considerably. This was a bit of a problem in the kitchen as clean dishes were often returned in error to upper cupboard shelves. "How was the party?"

"Most of the staff from the bakery department were there, and some of the girls from the deli and floral sections, too," said Peter. "Monica came with her husband and kids, so they moved us from the pub to the restaurant part."

"Yeah, Kelly and I arrived just after they'd moved the group, as did the department manager, so he helped us find the party," said Lisa. "It was a good-sized group, and they were all saying they would miss Peter and what a great guy he is."

"Lots of joking around," added Peter. "They liked my countdown poster." A quiet and softspoken man with dark hair that denied greying and ruddy brown eyes that hinted at his Metis heritage, Peter was a constant source of "dad jokes" and pun-filled silliness.

Some grocery store employees had arranged a pub night send-off for Peter after his last working day. He was officially retired. Part of him was sad to lose contact with these people, many of whom he'd known for the previous fifteen years. Still, he was tired of the politics and constant procedure changes of life during a pandemic. Grocery stores were deemed an essential service, and that had garnered a two-dollar-per-hour hazard pay bonus for a while and then points on their company reward cards instead. He was unimpressed. They were working full-time in an environment where customers grew progressively more irrational. Additionally, one had to constantly wonder if today would be the day you'd test positive for COVID-19. All of this added so much stress.

Lisa's last year before retiring had been working onsite in an office building with most other staff allowed to work from home. It was quiet, and she could focus on her work. Then, the rules changed, and other team members returned to the office. The anxiety was so intense that interactions were edgy with cleaning protocols, mask and cleaner supplies being challenging to acquire, and those damn directional arrows on the floor throughout the building. They'd all been there when she was alone, but *now* one had to actually follow them. Then, in her last month, she tried to get loose ends tied up and train a replacement who was not overly responsive to Lisa's training style. Covid restrictions meant that after over 20 years, her retirement party was a Zoom call and a basket of goodies; delightful, nonetheless. She was exhausted from the experience of working in government by her last working day. She fully understood Peter's relief and sadness. It was a kind of grief to end a career and an exciting pending adventure simultaneously.

Karl was younger than the others and would not retire for some time. He was of a more husky build with an avid interest in sports of all kinds and semi-pro experience in hockey. His thinning grey hair and thoughtful, highly observant manner was suited to his primary vocation of event security at a local arena. The job had varied hours, sending him to other venues with the same subcontracted service provider. He also had a side gig of live-streaming his gaming and tech skills. He worked with Lisa on her live-streaming project and repaired computers for family members and friends. His streaming was doing very well, and he had several sponsors. This was his passion, and all paid and volunteer skills and experience culminated in each video posted.

The big plan for Lisa had been to write books and travel. Unfortunately, Covid restrictions blew the trips out of the water. Travel outside the country, province or even health region jurisdiction at one point. Europe was her preferred destination, and that wasn't comfortably available yet. At least through live-streaming, she was able to connect with people worldwide, particularly other writers. Her Writers' Open Mic segments were growing in popularity. She loved encouraging others to share their work and talking about the processes of writing and publishing. The problem was her focus. Working from home was not a good fit for Lisa. She struggled with weight, and physical fitness in a home gym with limited social interactions was counterproductive. Returning via a short-term contract in a different government office was less about income than shaking her body's atrophy. She'd regained some focus with deadline pressures imposed by the new workplace.

Peter didn't have a big plan. He would relax when the pension income was established and then worry about budgets and what to do with his free time. But Peter knew that adding some hockey-playing sessions was on his agenda. He and Karl both played with an older beer league team. Both were goalies, and both loved the game and discussed improvements to technique until Lisa's eyes rolled back in her head. She was, though, their greatest fan and cheerleader.

"What do you want to do with your time now?" asked Karl. "You could come to work with us on a casual shift. We always need people."

"That might be a good idea. I would have some extra cash and still have time to fix stuff around here," Peter said thoughtfully.

"I still want to travel, and the sooner, the better," said Lisa, who had many travel websites bookmarked on her computer and mooned over them regularly.

Peter thought travel would be enjoyable, but the cost was dissuading. Karl wanted to start with an Alaskan cruise and short-term vacations as his work schedule permitted. The menfolk liked camping and often considered buying an RV to drive across Canada. Lisa was more of a glamping or cottage kind of person. Lisa wanted to find her family roots in Scotland and Ireland and attend art festivals. Book tours to various conventions and conferences were also on the list—a mix of historical sites, museums, and personal appearances in a lengthy vacation.

Dreams were good things to have, and moving those dreams into reality was something Lisa had the drive and stubbornness to achieve. Shoestring budgets and research had worked together to publish books and create memorable events successfully. That focus had helped her arrange a family trip to Mexico effectively just before the pandemic. Lisa knew it would all fall into place at some point.

"I'd like to get married. I love you guys, and we've been together for years. But, sometimes, it feels important to make it official and celebrate how lucky I am to be so loved."

"That's not going to happen," said Karl, patting her hand.
Both men were legally married to estranged spouses, while Lisa was divorced. Canadian law would only allow monogamous marriages. So a trio couldn't achieve this dream – well, her dream. Today, she wanted to express her love for them like any other woman, and her heart froze in disappointment. It might be legal elsewhere in the world, but that didn't change the issue at home.

Peter told Karl of the conversations at the party, and they laughed together. Lisa watched them and smiled on cue, but her mind was wrapped around the problem. An ineffective ice pick was working on her heart, chipping away at disappointment as it melted into sadness.

Twenty years with Peter, ten of which with Karl as a co-partner in spirit but single or separated legally. She sighed deeply, and the discontent pulled up from her toes, causing her to shudder. Both of Lisa's parents had passed away in quick succession, leaving her and a brother who lived thousands of miles away to resolve their estates and deal with their sentimental hoarding. She had been overwhelmed sorting through grief and legalities.

Lisa was acutely aware of the fragility of the human lifespan. Every thought was *how this would be achieved in whatever short time she now had to do it and what to do if she had to do it without them.* Her retirement bucket list was lengthy and currently seemed impossible.

Chapter Two

Lisa swiped her pass card, and the building door swung open. She shifted her laptop bag on her shoulder and adjusted the fit of her medical mask. She liked the reusable cloth masks better, but they were not as effective as the medical quality one-use masks, and of course, the N95 was the best sort. The masks, even when worn all day, weren't much of an issue for her, but it made wearing her glasses complicated. Do you pull the nose grip tight, prop your glasses over it, and hope the breath escaping doesn't fog them up, or wear the glasses only when not wearing the mask? She only needed them for distance and fogged up; they were useless, so she just left them in her purse. Eyestrain at her computer station was more of an issue. Her glasses were blue-tinted for that; fortunately, unless someone came to her desk to chat about something, she was okay to be maskless there.

Arriving at her floor, she located a workstation that was not in use and set her bags on the chair. Most staff were not assigned a workspace but had to share a large area of tables, chairs and monitors. They all had laptops and worked remotely from home, with several days weekly in the office. There were no desktop computers anymore – everyone was mobile. Most meetings were online video call formats. Extra work went into making verbal connections with co-workers to alleviate the isolation infiltrating the pandemic work culture. Every staff member had a signed agreement on where and when they would work and a process for reporting and advising of progress on their workload.

Lisa worked from home on Mondays and in the office for the rest of the week. Much of what she did involved boxes of paper files, which wasn't reasonable to transport home. It was good to have one day free of paper dust and work remotely in the software to catalogue the files. Lisa liked the work as it was second nature to her after all these years and a bit mindless. She could be lost in her thoughts or listen to music and still whip along in the process.

Lisa used the handy spray bottle of cleaner and paper towels to wipe down the desk, monitor and chair. The room was filling quickly with staff, and most workstations were occupied. Some greeted each other pleasantly and chatted to catch up. Others focused on getting set up as Lisa had done. Lisa loved listening to the chatter around her as so many languages were represented among her co-workers. She could recognize French, German, Spanish, and the cadence and charm of several others. These were possibly languages of the Middle East, Asia, and some local Indigenous dialects. Lisa studied several languages and linguistics at university, hoping to be a United Nations interpreter. She could understand more than speak any of them these days, however.

The laptop was set up, and all cords were connected; Lisa put on her mask and walked to the kitchen area. She slipped around a cluster of women chatting and made herself a nice hot cup of tea. Lisa greeted familiar faces, waving one hand and steadying her tea with the other. Returning to her desk, she tucked an earbud into each ear and pressed play on her phone's music app. Opening her email, she read each item and made notes on her notepad, creating a list of priority items, and then set to work on them.

Anastasia Guerriano, a lovely mature woman with a stylish updo and prim business suit, stood a few feet away, ambling along a row of short lockers, watering the plants in pots queued up on top. She appeared focused on her task but noted her staff's punctuality, attendance in general and seating choices.   She preferred to approach an employee's desk with questions; if there was a delay in an instant message or email response, it was necessary to note where they were sitting. This mobile sit where you want business was annoying. And trying to keep track of which staff were working remotely on any given day – just a nightmare. Thanks to Covid.

Anastasia stood on the tiptoes of her sensible pumps and plucked the dried remains of blossoms from the last plant. Then, she crumpled them in her hand and slid them into her jacket pocket. No garbage cans anywhere. Another efficient decision by the *powers that be* was cutting back on janitorial services and having only one central garbage and recycling container sorting system in the kitchen. She was reminded that she had an apple core on her desk, stowed the watering can on a shelf at the end of the row of lockers and walked into her office. As an Executive Director, Anastasia had an assigned space and a door to close for privacy. Closing that same door, she sat in her designated chair in her assigned office. The ED dropped the floral remains into the unassigned but stylish garbage canister under her desk to keep the apple core company until after her online meeting. She signed into her computer and logged into the meeting software.

"Good morning. How is everyone today?"

Luc Morneau and Giselle Leblanc chatted together at Giselle's desk. At the same time, Luc leaned closer, and Giselle pointed at her computer screen. They were excitedly working on a report for their research and development project team. One could almost see the lightbulbs going off over their heads.

"Ahh...regarde! Nous pouvons déplacer ce paragraphe vers le haut et mettre le tableau ici," Giselle said, poking at the screen.

"Oui! Cela fontionnera parfaitement," agreed Luc.

Luc returned to his workstation one table away and began typing with emphasized keystrokes and nervous mumbling. Giselle slid a headset over her ears and logged into the meeting software. Luc followed suit after turning to meet Gisele's gaze and giving her a thumbs up.

In a room next to the kitchen, Samantha Mah, the young office manager, sorted through a delivery of office supplies. Boxes of printer paper were piled high in a pyramid of potential. She sorted through another large box filled with pens, notepads, tape, and other essentials to the cogs of the wheels of business. Samantha consulted her clipboard and checked items off the packing list from the box. She observed that some things had been back ordered and were not in the box.

"Always the things you most need," she sighed and returned to her desk to delegate dispensing the supplies throughout the office.

* * *

Downstairs, exiting the ground floor lobby, Bert Fitzgibbons zipped up his official jacket with SECURITY in bright yellow on the back and began to tour around the building, checking doors and ensuring the security of the property. Then, finally, he turned a corner and found himself face to face with an eight-point buck.

"Well, there, buddy...what are you doing now? Did you want to speak with the boss?" said Bert, chuckling.

A significant parkland was a few blocks from the building, and it was not unusual to see deer wandering through the parking lot or along the street. However, they rarely came down the steps and into the lower walkway close to the building. The animals are used to people and have no fear, not even of vehicles, but keep their distance as a rule.

The deer snorted and tossed its head. It appeared to Bert that the animal wasn't sure how to get out of this area of the property. Bert used something between sign language and a rendition of a music video by Weird Al Yankovic to direct the animal to a quick escape path. Bert looked about with embarrassment and was glad the deer didn't have a phone to record that. The buck looked at him with fascination, snorted again and followed the directions. The buck wandered down the street toward the parkland, and the security guard whistled as he returned to his duties.

Chapter Three

Several blocks away in the inner-city park, under a tree on the far side of the first walking bridge that crossed over the river winding through the park, the fire department was hosing down the remains of a tent. It was a bit of a challenge to get to the fire as the city had closed all the roads in the park this past year. In addition, there was a constant struggle to keep the park safe and free of homeless encampments that seemed to attract a violent criminal element.

Roger Swartz shook his head, causing his helmet to bobble. He was not sure closing the roads off was the way to do it. Clearly, encampments were still a thing, and this one had burst into flame. Roger advised two other firemen, Calvin Smith and Ernie Werther, that the blaze appeared out. He poked around in the debris of the tent to ensure that there were no hot spots. Calvin shovelled out the shopping cart with the same intent. Then, the police and fire investigation team could take over the site. Roger's shovel hit something hard. He leaned over and pushed away some charred debris. Steam rose as the heat met the frigid winter air.

"Hey, Cal? You wanna get the cops over here?" called Roger.

"What's up?" returned Calvin.

"You want more water?" called Ernie. "I can reconnect the hose right smartly."

"Nope. I think we have a *Deceased Person*."

Officer Henry Zajic was speaking with Fire Marshall Hugh Logan in hushed tones. The cause of the fire was not immediately apparent. No lightning storms this time of year. And the snowfall had likely contained the fire's spread. Instead, a human cause was more likely – a kerosene heater, candles, or cigarettes - maybe someone just trying to keep warm.

"Very lucky that not much grass or underbrush was involved due to seasonal moisture. This could have been much worse at another time of the year," said Logan

Standing within earshot, Officer Ira Goldie bit his lower lip to suppress a giggle. The old fireman had such a knack for stating much of no consequence and was an expert at media diversion.

"Marshall Logan! Swartz found a *DP.*" Calvin interrupted urgently.

Officer Zajic nodded to Goldie, and they followed Firefighter Calvin Smith through the campsite debris. Tent and shopping cart on its side, charred items vaguely recognizable splayed across the ground. *Odd, the cart was on its side and not tarped in the tent area.* Officer Goldie examined the cart and asked the firemen, "Was this tarped in or against the tent, or did it get thrown over here as you put out the fire?"

"It was lying on its side, engulfed in flames when we arrived. I'm not sure if the tent caught first or the cart, but we didn't move it. Same with the personal effects - they were already tossed around the area. There could have been a fight, but that's not uncommon in this volatile group. They fight each other and themselves. Fire Marshall's team has to complete their investigation. Still, I don't see a kerosene heater or stove as a potential incinerate," Firefighter Roger Swatz responded thoughtfully.

Office Zajic had seen some nasty scenes in his 26-year career but never quite got over the smell of burned flesh. Of course, he knew that scent and didn't need to step closer, but as he did, he was saddened by the final moments of this life, underscored by the arms held over their head. Obviously, they felt afraid and alone. As he toured around the outer edges of the fire site, Officer Goldie noted large animal footprints in the snow with dragging marks leading further into the park. He made notes in his notebook and waved to his co-worker.

Officer Zajic reached for his radio mic. "Dispatch? We need the coroner's office to attend. We have one *Vital Signs Absent.* Ambulance not required."

The two police officers pursued the footprints into the woods. Meanwhile, the fire investigation team continued processing the scene, and the coroner's office reached the site. Finally, the firefighters packed up their equipment.

* * *

Sam piled several bags and packs next to a tree and pulled three sweaters tightly around their shivering body. The freshly gifted toque and mitts were toasty. Sam watched from a distance and mourned a friend. Tears froze on their cheeks, but the shudders that responded to shock more than temperature warmed them in a way. They'd been sick and spent the night at the shelter to get some cold medicine and a good night's sleep. Old Jacob had understood and said he'd be fine as usual.

"Nah...get out of de wedder and git well. Winter is mild in dis part of de country mais it is still cold on de bones and easy for sniffles to turn into sometin' muss worse."

Jacob was nearly 70 years old and had been on the streets for decades. Experience kept him safe and sheltered every night. Camping in the park was like a luxury hotel to the older man. Sam felt better this morning and, along with the toque and mitts, took some extra donuts from the breakfast buffet at the shelter for their friend. Jacob had a sweet tooth and loved baked goods, however stale.

When Sam arrived at the park and looked around for Jacob's campsite, they saw the flames. The fire truck came screaming into the park, but the camp was fully burning. Sam sat by the tree, too shocked to do more than watch it all, hoping to see that the firefighters had rescued Jacob. Unfortunately, no ambulance came, and there was no glimpse of Jacob or anyone else.

It must be Jacob's tent, and that sure looks like his cart, *thought* Sam with a moan of despair. Last summer, Jacob had taken Sam under his wing when no one else understood. He was kind and asked no questions, nor did he judge.

Tired deep in their soul, with arms folded on their knees, Sam put their head down on their arms and sobbed. The hardships of homelessness and the loss of the only thing that gave them hope – friendship – were overwhelming.

The squeak of a shopping cart with one wonky wheel approached on the street just over the hill. Sam gathered themself up and ran to the sound.   Jacob was plodding along, pushing a rusty shopping cart containing all his earthly possessions. The old man looked up, and seeing his friend, he grinned and waved.

"How are you feeling, Sam? Were the ladies at the shelter good to you?"

Sam ran up to Jacob and hugged him like a long-lost brother. Jacob laughed and pushed them off.

"Where dem goodies, or did you eat dem all?" he said, shaking a finger at his young friend.

"Well, if you're here, who's in your tent over yonder?" asked Sam, handing Jacob two sprinkled donuts.

"Ma tent was jacked," said Jacob, patting his cart's far side. The straps that had held an orange tent and blue tarp hung limply on the outside of the cart. "Some assholes snagged it when I was having a piss last night—rummaged through ma stuff too. So, I camped over to de ledge lawn wi' two filles from de mainland. Des saw de guys rip me off and wanted to be sure I was warm. Des had lovely wine and some good stories to share."

"Cops won't let you camp on the parliament building lawn," said Sam, puzzled.

"Des do if yer a protestor and causing a ruckus. Most fun I've had in years." Jacob raised his fists high and shouted, "SAVE THE OLD GROWTH!"

Sam was grateful for their friend's good fortune but wondered about the fire. Perhaps the dude who stole Jacob's tent had fallen asleep smoking in the tent. On the other hand, maybe it wasn't Jacob's tent. All he'd seen were flames, a pile of burnt stuff, and a shopping cart. It could be anybody, really.

The two wandered off together along the streets, with Jacob stopping now and again to raise his fists and shout, "SAVE THE OLD GROWTH." Sam would raise their fists and yell, "STOP CLIMATE CHANGE." Then, they would laugh and walk some more.

Chapter Four

Karl checked the pockets of his black cargo pants, looking for keys, wallet, earpiece, and other essential items. He zipped up his jacket and slung a duffle bag over his shoulder. He preferred to keep the company jacket and hat in his bag until on-site arrival. Patrons on the bus could get aggressive, especially young, entitled males looking to cause trouble. He'd prefer to listen to his music and have a prework Zen moment, then verbally joust with some dumbass. People, in general, had lost their ability to interact socially politely since being locked down during the worst days of the pandemic. Older folks were grumpier, and younger people were more verbal typically. Still, the influence of isolation and internet privacy had ramped things up. He also saw it in himself—less tolerance for stupidity and rudeness.

Slipping out the front door, he locked it and began the walk to the bus stop. It was a lovely walk along the private driveway of the townhouse complex. The river ran along one side, and geese clustered along the shoreline and often on the road, but not so much this time of year. Most of them had gone south for the winter. He selected a playlist and matched his stride to the music's baseline. His work boots crunched in the snow, and soon, he was at the top of the hill and onto the next street. It was an excellent warm-up walk for his work at the arena. Karl was more concerned about his health lately as he'd been diagnosed with lymphoma and had a tumour in his upper bowel. He had been worried that chemo treatments would not allow him to work, but the once-a-month therapies and recovery weeks between had fit nicely around his shifts. His boss was supportive, and so far, so good. Today, he was a bit nauseous, but otherwise, he felt fine.

Arriving at the bus stop, he checked his watch and looked at the posted *Active Schedule* or, as he called it - *Approved Suggestion* - which he determined was more accurate. Karl paced back and forth and then tossed his duffle bag on the bus shelter bench. Something fell under the seat, and the movement caught his eye before he heard a clunk of metal on concrete. It was a good-sized brass key. Not the type of thing you'd use for a padlock, but the old-fashioned sort for a keyhole in a door or drawer. Karl picked it up and measured its weight in his hand.

"Hmm. Quite hefty. I wonder what this is for," he said to no one in particular.

Several other people had assembled in and around the bus shelter. And some looked his way, nodded, shook their heads, or shrugged. An elderly lady had just arrived and settled on the bench beside his bag.

"Looks like the key to some girl's heart to me," she said, nodding to confirm this was the answer. She adjusted her thick glasses and blinked at him.

"Uh-huh. Well, I best keep it until I find her, don't you think?" Karl smiled at the woman. She looked intensely into his eyes, and he felt a tickle behind his forehead. That was weird.

"It's not a new woman. You've got enough women in your life. You need to make good with the ones you have; that key is important to one of them."

"Ah, what?" he stammered. The woman had gotten up and moved onto the bus with the others. He hadn't noticed the bus arriving. When he got on the bus, he looked for the woman, but the bus crowd prevented him from getting close enough to pursue the conversation. *Doing so would probably require a babel fish*, he thought.

He took his seat and went back to his tunes. Later, he would remember the key and find it safely in his pocket. In short order, Karl was entering the arena's staff entrance and chatting with co-workers.

The arena complex included an office building, a hotel, a casino, and a restaurant. The main arena bowl could be modified into a theatre space, ice rink, or basketball court as events required. Tonight was a punk metal concert, and the floor space was general admission with seating. Fans of the group would expect a mosh pit. Karl was usually assigned to supervise the front stage area where the guards caught the crowd surfing patrons and ensured their safety. Or tried to. Health order restrictions had just loosened to allow limited activities. Unfortunately, moshing was not one of them. So, the floor was filled with seats, and someone else would supervise fewer guards enforcing this event's current mask and seating protocol.

"oh...yippy skippy," said Karl as he listened to the staff briefing. Then, masked up and with gloves on, he and an event services staff member monitored one of the entrances and braced for admission of ticket holders. Finally, the four doors in the front foyer of the arena opened simultaneously.

Busy with his work, he did not notice what was happening at other doors until he heard a commotion. Three doors over, Ray Shannon, another security guard and Manjeet Singh, the event services person scanning tickets at that door, were engaged with five or six customers, all wearing full pale green masks of alien faces as you'd see in a B-movie.

The arena manager stood off to the side watching, and Karl laughed at the expression on her face. The cartoon speech bubble over her might have said, **"WTF?"**

A two-person security roaming team arrived with the security supervisor. The ticket holders were persuaded to use Health Officer-ordered masks under the alien faces, and the ingress proceeded smoothly. There were always people who wanted to bring cigarettes, alcohol, drugs, and food into the arena. None of these were permitted, and the refuse canisters swelled with discarded contraband.

"*Throw it out, put it in your vehicle, or go home,*" the guards would say. Of course, smoking was not permitted in the building. Experience told them that if they had them, they'd light up in the washrooms or stairwells because the other mantra of this security position was, "*Sorry, there's no re-entry allowed.*" (Point to sign above.)

It was a bit of a game to see what they could get past the guards, Karl thought, but went with the assumption that they didn't know the items were taboo and hadn't read multiple signs, the back of their tickets or the notice on the arena's ticketing website. It was a roll of the dice as to how these events went and whether patrons could cohabitate in the entertainment space happily. The likelihood of scuffles amongst patrons increased dramatically as the alcohol was served. Delays in the band, long lineups for refreshments, and testy interactions in the seats were all triggers. Some bands that appealed to older patrons frequently had fights in the seating sections over attendees dancing in their rows and blocking the view of those behind them. Younger patron groups were drug and alcohol-inspired nightmares.

Once most patrons had entered the building, Karl took his turn roaming with Daniel Van Kessel, a middle-aged guard who had to be close to seven feet tall and of broad build. They toured around the building, watching for trouble, checking locked doors and ensuring smoke-free washrooms.

"Can we get a roaming team up in the suites?" sang out a voice on their radios.

"22, here, Karl and I can swing by--which suite?" responded Daniel into his radio mic.

"18 – some issue with food service staff and a patron, not the suite owner," replied the voice. That would be Cindy Yellowbird, the event staff supervisor.

"Okay. We're on it." Daniel clipped the mic back on his shirt collar.

They took the elevator to the third floor and proceeded to Suite #18. They knew where to go by experience, but the sound of distressed voices would have been an excellent directional device.

"Well, sir, I can't wave my magic wand and make your credit card work!"

"Thanks, bitch. I get that. Why can't you charge it to the suite account for now?"

Karl and Daniel shared a look and turned the bend of the hall to see a group of patrons surrounding a food service person who was protecting a trolly of food items from hungry hands. Several suite doors were open, and curious patrons were standing by.

"Good evening, Sir. May we be of assistance?" offered Daniel. The security guard's considerable presence usually had a unique calming effect on riled-up people. Karl noted that #18's guest pulled himself up to his full 5'10 frame and bristled. Karl also observed that the female audience settled down in this encounter with wide eyes. Daniel smiled and nodded at them, and they giggled.

"He wants me to charge this to his suite, but I can't," said Tanisha Jackson, a very new food service staff person. "The owner of a suite must approve any charges."

"That is correct. And I am the owner of the suite." Julia Strauss of Strauss Solutions stepped into view from the other end of the hallway. She motioned for the others to go back into the suite. Then, pointing at the patron causing the dispute, she said, "Not you, Tim."

Turning to Tanisha, she pulled a wallet out of her handbag and handed a credit card to the young woman. Transaction completed; the food was wheeled into the suite.

"Mmmmhmmmph," said Tanisha to Tim as she passed him and gave him a look that would peel paint. Karl coughed, caught her eye, shook his head slightly, and opened the suite door wider for the trolley. Customer service being essential.

"Do you need anything further from us?" asked Daniel.

"Yes, would you be so kind as to escort Mr. Mansfield out of the building?" she said and turned to the man, who looked defeated and embarrassed. She held out her hand and said, "Ticket, please."

Tim Mansfield surrendered his ticket and entered the suite foyer to collect his jacket. "Using the suite is a privilege, and disrupting the arena staff is unacceptable. I'm sorry to take up your time, gentlemen."

Seeing that the excitement was over, patrons from other nearby suites returned to their activities. Karl and Daniel escorted their charge down the elevator and out the VIP entrance without further incident.

"I wonder what working for her is like?"

"She seems as though it would take a lot to rattle her. Very impressive."

"I wish all the suite owners would be alert to issues with their guests. Those food service people take a lot of crap."

"So do we. Remember when the cable company suite guests got boozed up and climbed into the upper bowl seating? Ninja jerks climbing all over seats and patrons but never dropped their beers."

The two men laughed and resumed their rounds patrolling the building.

* * *

Finding his car keys, Tim selected "open" on his fob and noted the click of the locks. He opened the door, slid into the driver's seat, and hesitated for a few minutes, one foot still on the pavement. Finally, Tim pulled himself into the seat and closed the car door. He was more annoyed than embarrassed by the encounter with his boss. He knew he was close to the limit on his credit card but hadn't counted on hungry women. He'd hoped it would clear anyway. Julia could be a real cow sometimes, but that had been mild for her. She tolerated Tim for the most part for his professional expertise, but it was clear that she wasn't a fan of his fantastic charisma. Neither was Marina, the very hot woman in the front office, his special guest tonight. She'd accepted his invitation on behalf of the entire front office staff. Not what he'd intended. *Smart little cookie, he thought. I should be glad she didn't invite my wife too.* Tim signed and started the engine.

* * *

Back in the suite, Marina Caravalho and Lucy De Sousa clinked glasses and giggled. The twin sisters had worked together at Strauss Solutions for six months. Lucy had been employed there for several years. She recommended her sister's secretarial skills to Julia when that position opened up. Marina and Lucy were both single, but each had been in a previous relationship, which resulted in a child. Lucy monitored account receivables and collections, while Charlotte Fischer handled accounts payable and payroll. Elias Fischer was the comptroller. He and Charlotte had been married for ten years and had a son. Tonight, they had shared babysitters with Lucy and Marina – Julia's teenage daughter and her friend were managing a sleepover event of small superhero dudes involving video games, movies and junk food.

Julia thought that Tim's marketing and client sales skills were essential to the success of her business; however, she was a bit tired of his overt and frankly harassing conduct, which had grown in frequency lately. Lucy had been a target briefly, but not long as her collection work was a natural fit. She shut down aggressive conversations and behaviour instantly. Carmen Sam, unfortunately, quit her secretarial position to get away from him. Julia wished she had been alerted to it sooner, although there wasn't much to be done without official complaints.

Tim had been with the firm for five years. While he'd always been a bit overly friendly with females, it wasn't until a year ago that he became a problem. She wondered what was going on in his marriage that Tim felt such a need for control – that's what it amounted to - a power struggle, not an actual interest in cheating. He seemed to enjoy offending women – including getting called on the carpet for it. *Troubling,* thought Julia, feeling quite helpless and ineffective. *It was a bit ironic that Strauss Solutions had no solution.*

Julia sampled a basket of nachos and sipped the straw on a can of pop. She'd like to think she was a decent employer and the staff felt appreciated. Then, smiling at her team, she raised her drink to toast them. They responded and continued chatting over the music and dancing.

* * *

On the other side of town, three sleepy superheroes were tucked into a blanket fort and sung to sleep by two teenage girls and a guitar. They whispered over the music and slipped into dreams of dastardly villains bested.

Chapter Five

Peter had been working around the house, catching up on repairs and laundry for the most part. He watched a movie and thought about dinner preparations. Then, he left the house with big garbage bags filled with empty cans and pop bottles. He tossed them in the van to deliver to his favourite recycling depot. Peter drove along the community road and waved at other tenants walking along the way.

Jalissa Williams waved to Peter through the windshield of her car as she passed his van on the narrow drive, which was made more limited by parked cars and snow piles. She parked her car in her spot and began unloading grocery bags. *Bembe would be avoiding his homework with that bloody gaming again. Cai Hong did not dissuade him from skylarking.* She clucked her tongue and shook her head.

Jalissa set her bags down and unlocked the door of her townhouse. Swinging it wide to enter, she called out, "Bembe! Ronica! Come help yer Mama wi' de bags!"

"Mi soon come!" called her son from a distance.

"Bloody video games," Jalissa grumbled.

"Wah Gwaan, Mama?" Ronica appeared in the front hallway, her braids swinging as she walked. Jalissa noted that her daughter was blossoming and would need a mother's counsel soon. Two years older than her brother, she would start high school in the fall. Jalissa sighed. They grew up so very fast.

Soon, the groceries were unpacked, and supper was in the works. Ronica chatted about her school trip to a rink for ice skating. She shared that many of her friends had toboggans and sleds. The weather called for more snow, and the kids were excited to enjoy the winter sports. Jalissa had no experience with winter sports or driving. Snow was not part of her Jamaican youth. Ronica's homework was completed, and her books had already been tucked into her backpack. She was a good girl.

"Bembe and Cai Hong were teasing the turtles again," whispered Ronica conspiratorially. "I snuck up and saw them."

"Doan be tellin' tales on yer brutha now," said Jalissa. "Dis Mama sees it all." She winked and patted her daughter's head.

Upstairs, she could hear the boys talking or reading aloud, which is how it sounded—both of them were good kids but put together – all kinds of trouble.

Cai Hong and Bembe Williams were best friends. They shared the same birthday and wore the same shoes, but discovering each other's family customs and languages was a long-standing shared interest. The kids had first met five years previously in kindergarten and had spent almost every day together since. Bembe's family had come to Canada from Jamaica, while Cai Hong's family was originally from China. They had embraced being different together.

Cai Hong lay on the floor, watching a turtle crawl on the rug. He used a chopstick to redirect it. Bembe poked at another turtle from his viewpoint a few feet away.

"Ya thinks they be fighting each other? We could make dem little poles."

"Sticks or swords? Maybe. Don't have toxic green goop."

"I got green slime. Dat works, yeah?"

"No. Need nuclear waste."

"ah...we could nuke it in de microwave!"

The turtles were shoved together but did not "rumble." The impact knocked one over on its shell, with feet flailing. The other had no compassion and went on its way.

"I tink Oscar gave up. And Myers doan care."

"Let's go play on QR 2."

The turtles were returned to their terrarium, and the kids bounced onto the end of Bembe's bed. He flicked on the gaming system, and the TV screen flashed bright images and then a black screen with a big yellow circle sad face.

"Oh, controller loose," said Cai Hong. After a bit of scrambling, the bright screen returned. Images flashed in a split-screen two-player mode, and soon, avatars were revised for battle. Shooting stars, flying dragons and a map full of notations for quests appeared. They must fight to find the princess in the tower and beat off monsters and evil warriors.

Bembe's avatar was a male Elf Warrior with a crossbow and arrows. He wore leather armour, danced when prompted and had a horrible aim. Cai Hong's avatar was a female Mountain Ogre with metal armour, a long stick with a hooked end and much better aim. She saved the princess, and suddenly, the screen showed hearts dancing around a rainbow.

Bembe's mom called to say that supper would be ready soon, so they quickly turned off the game and pulled their homework out of their backpacks. Then, stretching out on the rug, they organized themselves to look fully engrossed in their studies. In truth, there wasn't much to do that couldn't be managed at lunch recess the next day. Bembe had some math to finish, and Cai Hong wanted to read more about today's science lesson. They also had to practice their lines for the school play.

Ronica stood in the hallway, listening at the bedroom door. Then, finally, she knocked loudly on the door, enjoying the sounds of scuffling on the other side.

"Come down for supper, now. Mama sez, you've studied long enough and must be starving." She snickered as the door opened, and the younger children bolted out of the room and down the stairs. She glanced into the room and shook her head. Books lay open, pencils discarded, and questions were left hanging in the air.

A few minutes was long enough for any ten-year-old kid to want to study, Jalissa thought, noting how happily the pair appeared at their dining table. But Bembe would show her precisely what studying was left pending before bed. Cai Hong's parents would likely do the same when he went home after their meal.

Jalissa smiled to herself as hungry children were too busy to say much. She was happy to work long hours at the hospital, picking up extra shifts. The Covid times had been exhausting, and while everyone hoped that life could go back to normal, the news was full of predictions of more and worse. She felt it best to focus on today and tuck away funds and supplies in preparation.

Ronica and the boys cleared their plates and put them in the dishwasher while Jalissa washed the pots and pans. Then, there was a knock at the front door, and it immediately opened.

"Cai Hong! Your daddy is here, boy. Come with yerself!" A tall black woman wearing a leather jacket, tweed pants and an orange knit slouch cap entered the townhouse, followed by a shorter Asian man in a business suit.

"Tanisha! Yuh nuh ave a shift at di arena tonight?" said Jalissa, entering the front hall.

"No, girl. That shift was cancelled. Some shit going down with that place lately. Good, I have my other job," said Tanisha Jackson as she dropped her backpack in the hall, hung her jacket in the closet and kicked her shoes off.

"Jù ba, érzi, wǒmen huí jiā ba, " said Wei Chan, stepping quickly past Tanisha and waving his arms about urgently at his son.

"Hǎo de, bàba. Wǒ qù ná wǒ de bèibāo," replied Cai Hong, running upstairs and returning with this backpack and jacket.

"Mi luv yuh wa suppa?" said Jalissa to the other woman.

"Sure, but a nice hot tea more," replied Tanisha, pulling a lunch bag out of her backpack.

Cai Hong and his father hustled out of the house. Jalissa noted that Ronica and Bembe also disappeared very quickly.

Tanisha sat at the dining room table while Jalissa made tea and a plate of warmed leftovers. The women chatted about the events of the day. Jalissa's 12-hour shift in the emergency ward was full of stressful moments. Tanisha worked in a bank as a teller and took hospitality shifts at the local arena. Working hard to save money and preparing for the future drove both women, inspired by childhood memories of extreme poverty.

Tanisha's mother had worked in the sex trade in East Vancouver from the age of fifteen. Raven had given birth to Tanisha at nineteen and disappeared just before her daughter's fourth birthday. Tanisha had been told that her father was "some black dude" from Seattle. She'd been in and out of foster homes and even stayed on a reserve with her mother's family for a while. Tanisha didn't fit in anywhere but finished high school and got a job cleaning at the Friendship Centre in Victoria. She'd been lucky to find some kindness there, and through that connection, she met the first employers who allowed her to prove her quick study and determined work ethic.

Jalissa had married out of poverty, and her husband's family was unimpressed. When she was widowed with two small children, her in-laws begrudgingly funded her immigration to Canada. They wanted nothing to do with her, but she did have an Auntie living and doing well in Vancouver. Jalissa was helped to get into nursing school and then went to work with her aunt.

"Ah, so, long day, but I am some glad that I dun have ta work tonight," said Tanisha, "but the extra bucks woulda been fine."

"Cum yah an mi wi kiss yuh sad face," said Jalissa, leaning across the table to deliver said kiss.

"Girl, we both got de night off – best be more kisses than for my sad black face!" Tanisha chuckled and returned the affection with interest.

"Mammmaaaaaa!"

Chapter Six

Delia stretched and rubbed her eyes. This article was going to have to write itself. Her mind didn't want to focus on the plight of random citizens and their heroic championing of various pandemic-impacted obstacles. Not today. Jet lag was not the issue; it was more of a need to process the frustration of her recent trip. She replayed the memory:

The airplane shimmied and shuddered in random spurts and really not that aggressively. Delia Ismat-Campbell knew that air travel was statistically safer than travelling by car. Still, she wondered if they stored parachutes somewhere on the plane like ferries stored life jackets. The stewardess showed the location of exits, oxygen masks, and life jackets for if the plane went down in the ocean, but there was no mention of jumping out of the aircraft in flight.

"Let's not get all twisted up, Delia," she said to herself.

"A bit nervous, are you?" said a voice across the aisle. Delia turned to see a middle-aged woman wearing a Hijab of soft mauve gauze fabric and a business suit of a different, more solid cloth – maybe linen – but of the same colour. On the lapel of her jacket was a large broach of a golden scarab.

"Yes. I don't know why as I've flown many times. But, today seems the day to be on edge, I guess," replied Delia.

"I have an app on my cell phone that plays soothing music and lets me drift into a peaceful meditation," the woman offered, "Would you like to use it?"

"I wouldn't want to impose..." said Delia.

"Not at all. Here you go," said the woman. "I am Fatima Al Taiir. Please enjoy."

"Shukran jazilan lak, Fatima. My name is Delia." She didn't speak Arabic but had learned some phrases and could at least be thankful.

After some instruction, Delia sat back in her seat and slipped on her earbuds. The music began with soft tones, and she drifted off.

After a few minutes of guided meditation, she found herself in a lush forest filled with birds, squirrels, and rabbits. It was so vivid that she could smell the soil and underbrush. Delia could hear the birds calling to each other, and she felt the chill of a breeze wrap around her body. She walked through the woods and came upon the crumbling tower of an abandoned castle. She was drawn to the building as a pin to a magnet. It had stone walls, and the floor was covered in mud, overgrown by vines. A large mural was painted on the wall with a deep brown paint that flaked off when she touched it. The mural was of a cluster of scarabs crawling over a person who held a clock - no, it was a stopwatch. Delia picked up flakes of paint and smelled them. The fragments did not smell of paint but appeared to be dried blood. The watch was stopped at 15 seconds.

Next, she felt a buzzing in her head like a bee had been trapped in her hair. Finally, Delia opened her eyes and found that the plane was nearing its destination. Returning the cell phone to Fatima, she thanked her again and said she felt very rested and relaxed.

The passengers disembarked from the plane, and Flight 1515 arrived in Riyadh. Delia adjusted the paisley print scarf around her head, ensuring it covered her hair and neck. She was looking forward to meeting her grandparents and Saudi family. Her adoptive parents were children of immigrants from Scotland and Saudi Arabia. They had given her a wonderful childhood; she loved them dearly and had never needed to know about her roots until her father passed away and her mother became ill. Then, suddenly, she felt like the two-year-old orphan they had brought into their home so many years before.

Her adoptive mother had always warned that the circumstances around her birth might be difficult and to try to understand if she was not well received. Letters had been exchanged, however, and a local contact - a friend of her adoptive father's family, was excited to meet Delia and help her find out more. But, unfortunately, she wasn't sure of anything beyond the fact that she'd been adopted from an orphanage in Riyadh. While the trip had been lovely in meeting her extended adoptive family, the orphanage records were either lost or destroyed, and the importance of record keeping regarding orphans evaded the regional office personnel. So she was no further ahead.

CRASH! "Oh, so sorry. Excuse me." The waitress had dropped a tray of silverware wrapped in paper napkins.

"No worries. Here, let us help you with that." Two patrons were helping to salvage any uncontaminated utensil packs.

Delia was startled from her memories and noted the time. She pulled out her earbuds and stopped the music app on her phone, thinking: *I must pack up and get moving shortly.* She hadn't made much progress on her article despite a looming deadline. Even her favourite 80s playlist hadn't given her the boost it usually did. Working remotely in a coffee shop or restaurant brilliantly met her nutritional and hydration needs, and this place was very cozy but distracting at the same time. It made her feel at home and very alone simultaneously. However, the dead end of limited orphanage records and a resulting sense of obscurity devastated the voice of her writing. Her thoughts kept pounding at that brick wall.

Draining her cup and setting her dishes in a pile on one side of the table, she looked around the café, noticing it was now busy. She had one last look through her email and shut down her computer. The waitress collected her dishes and tried unsuccessfully to coax Delia into having another Chai Latte.

She packed her things into a backpack and slipped in and out of the washroom before leaving the restaurant. Then, crossing the street outside the restaurant, she approached a set of Canada Post mailboxes and dropped a small white package in one of them. Delia paused to add a prayer for some direction from the pending analysis of her RelativeDNA sample to the parcel's postage.

Noting the overcast skies, Delia determined she might have enough time to take a shortcut through the park before nightfall. She wondered how the construction near the Children's Petting Zoo was going. Delia walked a bit faster to accommodate that detour. Perhaps that would be the angle her article needed.

A few minutes later, she found herself in a lush forest filled with birds, squirrels, and rabbits, much like the one in her meditation dream on the plane. However, Meeachan Park had highly manicured lawns, old-growth treed areas, and primarily squirrels, pond birds, and the odd deer lived there. She was viewing a pretty noticeable change, especially this time of year. Delia walked through the woods and found three or four young guys harassing some homeless encampment residents near the duck pond. They set a trashcan ablaze and shot firecrackers into the encampment.

Delia quickly hid in the underbrush and called 911 on her cell phone. The group seemed delighted with themselves and had no concern for the screaming children in nearby tents. They laughed more. The sounds of approaching sirens gave them pause, and they left the area. Delia chatted with some of the encampment residents. Several of them gave statements to the police, including a woman named Joy and her children, Paul and Nicole, while the fire department put out the trashcan. She had a direction for her article and some anger with the life and times of the city where she lived.

Chapter Seven

Peter Primeau tossed empty bags into the back of his van, having reclaimed the deposit on the pop bottles they contained. He was just shy of forty dollars to the better, which would go in the gas tank. So he stopped at his favourite station, topped up the van, and snagged a ticket for tonight's lottery. Peter didn't know what he'd do with a 70-million-dollar grand prize, but one of the smaller one-million-dollar prizes would do him just fine.

"This is a winning ticket, right?" he joked with the cashier.

Next, Peter stopped at a grocery store and picked up some milk and a few bits for dinner. He'd already set the pork ribs to marinating, and his mouth watered, thinking of the side dishes that would complete the meal. Peter's love language was food, and he happily searched for new ways to delight his family.

Stowing his purchases in the back of the van, Peter negotiated a nearby fast-food drive-through and ordered a root beer and fries. Pulling up to the pay window, he joked with the cashier and pretended to pay with a rewards points card. Then, pulling up to the takeout window, he joked again. Peter was a natural flirt and very devoted to it.

Back home, Peter guided the van into his parking spot and collected his purchases. Walking across the parking lot to their townhouse, he greeted neighbours, commenting that the little snow they'd received had nearly melted away. His phone rang as he put away purchases and puttered in the kitchen.

Noting the phone's display, Peter answered. "Hi, Mom! What's new?" Peter's mother and stepfather lived in another part of the province but maintained a close telephone relationship. Peter hadn't seen his mother in several years, partially due to pandemic restrictions and the complexity of his household's work schedules. Lately, it was a consideration as to whether the van would survive the trip without some extensive upgrades or if he should buy something newer. Retirement meant more time but less financial flexibility. After a brief but pleasant conversation, Peter returned to his puttering.

Peter chuckled to himself. He would always be her little kid in his cowboy outfit, complete with a hat and holstered six guns. Later, Peter would see himself walking in Batman's shadow, but when he was little, he liked the jingle of the spurs as he walked. It was almost as good as when he clothes-pinned playing cards to the front tire of his chopper bike with the banana seat and hot rod handlebars and tore down the street with a motorcycle soundtrack.

Peter checked the oven quickly and confirmed that supper was underway, then settled himself on his laptop in his easy chair. Scanning social media for new recipes, Peter found an exciting twist on a fish dish. Karl came into the house at that point, and the two men discussed employment opportunities for Peter with Karl's firm.

"The company will give you a uniform shirt, but you'll have to provide your black pants and shoes."

"I have black cargo pants from my last job and black steel-toed work shoes, too."

"That will do. There are spare uniform shirts in the office at the arena. A flashlight and a multi-tool might be useful, though."

"Okay."

Karl coached Peter on where to apply online, and Peter completed that process. Then, Lisa bounded in the door, a veritable fountain of information. Social media was buzzing with details of fire and death in the city park's homeless population.

"Apparently, it could have been worse if the weather had been dryer, but they found someone's remains in the tent, so I'm sure that's bad enough," said Lisa, consulting new bits in her social media feed.

"Did they identify the body?" asked Peter,

"Coroner is likely working on it, " Karl also checked his social media feed.

"I thought the city had moved the homeless encampment out of Meeachan Park. When did they move back?" said Peter.

"I haven't seen many folks around my office building for weeks. It's been so cold, but I've heard that the shelters are over capacity most nights," commented Lisa.

"Says it was just the one tent involved, but the cops only move them out in the daytime. So they camp at night by the big totem pole on the south end," said Karl, tapping his iPhone screen.

"Well, that's good that there weren't more hurt, but still sad," Lisa said, peeking on dinner preparations and thinking about some work she needed to do in her home office.

Karl and Peter returned to their discussion, and Karl coached Peter through the company's website to submit his resume.

The plight of nameless, homeless people was a typical news item these days. Unfortunately, the answer seemed beyond the scope of the politicians and non-profits mandated to find solutions. With rents skyrocketing, most people were a few wrong turns away from losing their housing and food security at any moment. Yet, these same folks tried not to think about it and avoiding the discomfort of being reminded prevented much more than annual donations or food bank collections.

Chapter Eight

The north end of Meeachan Park was once an ancient indigenous village. The foundations of some dwellings can still be seen. Burial cairns had been recovered in the park. The land, covered in blue Camas flowers every spring, remembers the villagers who gathered them centuries ago and speaks with a sacred hush to those who would listen. As a public trust property owned by the city, it is held in high regard amongst area citizens. So, it is no surprise that homeless humans and animals find comfort amongst the manicured lawns and old trees. The park has a cricket field, children's water park, gardens, fountains, and ponds that are full of life. To the south end of the park are foundations of a later Celtic settlement, near which a construction site for an expansion to the petting zoo had recently begun work. There is a well-maintained forested area between the zoo and the location of the tent fire. Close enough to hear the bleating of the goats and donkeys who resided in the zoo but far enough away to be somewhat hidden from public eyes.

Officers Goldie and Zajic strolled through the trees, following animal footprints and dragging marks in the snow-covered ground.

"I thought this might lead us to a friend of our DP, but I'm starting to think this is one big cat, and the dragging mark is its tail," said Goldie.

"I'd agree, even though the footprints initially seemed to come this way - there are bigger footprints for the last 20 feet going back the other way. Where did it go? And where is the bigger cat? Have we got *two* cougars in the park?" pondered Zajic.

The trails had gone cold as they approached the paved road between the forest and the petting zoo. The two men paused and looked around. It was getting dark quickly, and there didn't seem to be a solution to the mystery.

"We can't call in a cougar sighting without...an actual cougar sighting," said Goldie.

"What's that?" said Zajic, nodding toward the construction area.

A soft blue light was glowing and moving around as if someone were looking about with a flashlight.

"Could be a security guard," said Goldie. They looked at each other, nodded, and walked toward the light. Some excavation had been done to lay a foundation for a new building, perhaps a new barn. Several small buildings were already in the zoo to house the animals overnight, but they had to be fostered at local farms through the winter. So the Friends of Meechan Park had fundraised to build a larger winterized building to house them and double as a winterized education centre.

"Looks like they hit a snag with that boulder," said Zajic, his flashlight beam dancing over a large boulder in the excavated depths. A large blue tarp was affixed over one end of the hill's rock face at the dig's far end.

The tarp glowed back in response, one corner flapping in a breeze that wasn't felt by the men but might account for the movement they'd seen.

"Oh, now that's interesting," said Goldie, picking his way along the scaffolding and going into the dig site. He walked right up to the tarp and pulled up the loose corner.

"I don't think this is rock. This is manmade - it looks like wood under the clay and maybe straw. Like that Cobb stuff they built houses out of in the documentary I was telling you about. " he continued.

"Like terracotta clay?" offered Zajic

"Well, yeah, but mixed with straw and more substantial. See, there's clay mashed into this too, but if you pick at it, it's definitely wood sticks woven around tree brush under the clay."

The two investigated further, pulling back more of the tarp.

"Looks a bit like the entry to a Celtic Roundhouse. Have you seen the one in the museum? It has a thatched roof like that bit up there. Carvings and paintings on the walls inside and out," said Zajic.

"This one carving could be a raven or crow. And that looks like antlers on the left with a candle flame in the centre above the door.!" exclaimed Goldie. "This is an important find. I wonder if they've reported it to the city."

"Most likely - since the excavation was halted. We get so little snow that it would not have been a weather delay. Doesn't explain the light glowing, though." said Zajic as the light began to glow around the edges of the door and somehow through it.

"Maybe somebody figured out how to get in there."

The two men worked the tarp back further and found a piece of wood that had wedged the door slightly ajar. Pushing against the clay-covered wood, they slowly swung it open. The light was soft, but a frigid wall of air pressed against them, giving a physical underscore to the feeling that they were not welcome to enter.

Goldie was knocked back and found himself seated in the mud. Zajic held to the door frame, stood his ground for a few more seconds, and stepped back. Both were shaken by seconds that had felt like hours.

"Was that a wolf howling?" said Officer Goldie, looking back over his shoulder.

"We don't have wolves in the city. Probably a dog or some kid messing around," responded Officer Zajic absentmindedly. "Did you feel that...force field? Like the building didn't want us in there."

"Yeah. And I heard a voice. " whispered Goldie, still searching for the source of the howling that continued.

"I did, too. It said: *Nothing to see here. Move along, now. Go buy your wife some flowers and take that trip to Maui,*" said Zajic

"Oh. I heard: *Mind your own business. Find a different job where you find joy every day,*" said Goldie, getting to his feet.

"Did you recognize the voice?" asked Zajic, pulling the tarp back in place.

"Miss Sanderby, my first crush – school nurse," said Goldie. "Who did you hear?"

"Father Arnstone, my high school principal,' said Zajic.

"So what do we put in the report on this? Psychic meltdown?"

"No trespassers found?"

"Works for me."

The two men left the construction zone and paused briefly at the edge of the petting zoo parking lot while several cars passed them. Then, finally, they returned through the park to their cruiser.

Both men were still visibly shaken and found their minds filled with memories of the person attached to the voice and the message they had heard. Neither noticed that grass sprouted in the construction mud as they walked across it and that the undergrowth grew under the old trees as they passed by on their way back to their squad car. However, they did notice the remains of rabbits and squirrels at the base of an old bent Arbutus tree.

"Stop!" said Zajic, "Did you hear that?" He paused and looked up into the Arbutus tree.

"Hmmm," said Goldie, listening.

There was a low, deep rumbling.

"He just licked his lips and asked for a cop dessert," whispered Goldie.

"I consider that a cougar sighting," replied Zajic, walking slowly but steadily to the police vehicle.

Goldie didn't stop moving until he was in the car and the doors locked. Zajic called in the cougar, and they waited for animal control to arrive.

Chapter Nine

The following day, the sun came out to chase away the snow that had fallen during the night. The city's park maintenance crew arrived. As the fire investigation team had collected what they needed the previous day, city staff removed the remaining fire damage to the park grounds and waited for police to arrive. Every morning, the homeless encampment from the night before was required to pack up and move on until nightfall. The city was determined to keep the park garbage-free and maintained for everyone's enjoyment. City workers did not attempt clearing up until the police were present. Their collection of garbage was frequently met with aggressiveness otherwise. One person's trash was another's treasure and, most often, their only possessions holding space for a life's memories.

The construction site was muddy, but the crew wouldn't be digging today. Butch Henry, the owner of Henry Construction, had been onsite yesterday when the old village doorframe was discovered. His Indigenous-owned and operated business had won the contract to build for the Friends of Meeachan Park project. His crew feared proceeding anywhere in the dig site and disturbing the ancestors. Instead, he'd closed the site and tarped over the structure, leaving his brother Jared to guard against vandals. Jared was nowhere to be found this morning. The tarp had been pulled away, and Butch was concerned that Jared had encountered some trouble.

Butch stood at the edge of the dig site and watched as several vehicles approached and parked in the petting zoo parking lot. Two squad cars were already parked there while the police searched the area for Jared. Butch replaced the tarp and secured it before his visitors arrived.

Susan Ramirez, Director of Archaeological Acquisitions from the Royal Museum of British Columbia, whose exhibits included other artifacts from the park, got out of the first car along with Arnold Thomas from the World Religions wing of the museum. In another car, he could see Francis Charles and Cindy Malone, board members of the Friends of Meechan Park group. They joined the first group and greeted the others.

The third car was driven by Julia Strauss, who was accompanied by her sales guy - Tim something. Butch had contacted Francis yesterday and related the find. He was pleased to see museum representatives present. He hoped they could convince his crew that terrible punishments were not ahead for them. However, Butch was puzzled that Julia and Tim had decided to visit the site today. The Strauss Solutions company had sourced dump trucks for this project and helped find a larger excavator. Still, he hadn't asked for anything new, and the fee schedule had been met. Butch stepped forward and greeted each person respectfully, and answered their questions.

"We'd like to see the structure more closely. Is there a way down there that isn't climbing on a scaffold?'

"Absolutely. There's a ramp over there. Still a bit of a muddy climb, but not too steep."

The group moved to the ramp, which was made uneven by deep tire treads in the wet clay. However, the walk was less complicated than anticipated, and everyone had reassembled in front of the tarp in short order. Butch pulled back the tarp exposing a wooden door framed by wood-planked walls covered in clay and straw and a header of carved wood. The door, covered in mud, stood ajar. Above the door header, Butch noticed that a thatched roof was beginning to appear.

He heard gasps and "Oh my." Then, "How beautiful!" from behind him. Next, turning to look at the others, he saw tears and recognition in their eyes.

"Hmm...the carvings above the door could be a crow for The Morrigan, Anu's crown of horns on the other end – and in the middle is Brigid's Flame, wouldn't you say?" said Arnold Thomas, one well-versed in Celtic pantheons.

"Brigid is the Goddess of the Healing Waters, Sacred Flame and Fertile Earth. The Morrigan is associated with war and prophecy. She appears as a crow or wolf but can shapeshift into any animal. Finally, Anu is Goddess of Earth and Fertility." shared Cindy Malone, excitedly remembering the lore from her university studies. Arnold nodded and smiled.

"These carvings on the door are Pucas," said Arnold, rubbing mud away from two carvings. "The Pucas are mischievous changeling creatures that can transform into animal form and bring either good or bad luck," said Arnold, caressing the images with reverent fingers. "This is about transformation. Enter here, find what you need to heal, change, and transform into your best self."

"...,most fearsome self..." whispered Cindy, covering her mouth quickly in response to Arnold's frowning glance.

"The excavator struck the wood, and we continued with shovels to see what this was," said Butch. "The door frame was lying flat on the ground. My brother pulled mud out of the carvings and cleaned it up. Then I put a tarp over it to keep it safe while we finished digging the rest of the foundation area."

"Flat to the ground, you say?" asked Susan. "Did you prop it up against the structure later?"

"No, Ma'am. We took a lunch break and came back to find that the earth beneath it had risen a few feet such that the door frame was propped to a 45-degree angle," responded Butch. "It scared my crew, and that was the end of work for yesterday. Then, this morning, I found it as you see it."

As he spoke, clumps of earth and grass continued to fall away from the sides of what appeared to be a long and rounded thatched-roofed structure. Several people commented that the whole form had gotten taller since they first saw it, but they had also gotten closer to it. New grass sprung up in the mud under their feet.

"It is an amazing discovery. I'd like to see what is inside," said Susan, looking at Francis and Cindy, who nodded.

The museum and board members discussed this amongst themselves. They decided to thank the three goddesses and seek a blessing on the site. It was also determined that a Saining purification for each person before entry was necessary. Arnold's sing-song and heartfelt invocation was followed by Cindy lighting a bundle of juniper branches. She held it for each person in turn to pull the smoke of the singed juniper over their heads and body. Blessings were requested aloud and in whispers.

"It may need further excavation and some structural support, so please be careful, " Butch commented.

Butch pushed on the door and stepped aside for the others to enter. Susan entered first, taking the smoking juniper bundle from Cindy and waving it over the door's carvings and ahead of herself into the building.

Several of the others entered gingerly. Cindy paused and stood by Julia, placing a hand on her arm. "This is so exciting. I've never been this close to my ancestral teachings."

Julia nodded in agreement and advised that neither she nor Tim would intrude on this moment.

The others returned quickly, speaking in hushed but very excited voices. The building was vibrating and felt unsafe, but they had been excited by the interior carvings and paintings.

"This appears to be a Celtic roundhouse dedicated to healing. I'd guess the design of the High Middle Ages is 1000 to 1300 CE, tentatively - we'll have to investigate further to confirm authenticity. Of course, we'll need to be involved in any '*development,*' and this area should be restricted access," said Susan Ramirez.

"That's why I asked Julia and Tim to join us. Strauss Solutions' donations have greatly supported projects in the park. We want to negotiate funding to assist us in assessing this find."

"The Friends of Meeachan Park will want to work with the Royal Museum and the City of Victoria," said Cindy. The museum moved in recent years to develop traditional cultural exhibits, including an ancient Indigenous village and burial sites at the park's north end, in collaboration with the park's many associated partners.

"There are modern Celtic Shamans and followers in this area, but I don't know of any Brigid Flamekeepers in the city. However, Ord Brigadeach in Ireland will have a record and is sure to be interested in the spiritual context of this amazing structure," said Arnold.

"U Vic Archaeological Studies would likely want in as well. So there could be developmental funding sourced all over the place," said Tim.

All eyes were on Tim, and Julia sensed that the others had forgotten she and Tim were there.

Julia coughed. "I'm happy to support whatever process is agreeable to the Friends of Meeachan Park, and thank you so much for explaining these wonderful carvings. I can feel such peaceful energy here, almost a hushed embrace."

The group chatted a bit longer, moving toward their vehicles and finally leaving. Julia and Tim had remained near the structure, talking with Butch about how to move forward with construction and equipment that might be needed. They surmised that the Friends of Meeachan Park would have to revise their blueprints to accommodate what appeared to be an archaeological find or move the planned winterized barn to another part of the park. Pending that decision, Butch noted that his work was at a halt. He tucked the tarp back in place and secured it.

Julia and Butch discussed hiring an independent security firm to restrict access to the site rather than using his employees, given their reactions to the strange happenings here.

At that point, police arrived to advise that they had found Jared asleep on a bench in the entryway of the public washroom building on the other side of the park. He was okay but traumatized by a glowing white spirit – a screaming woman - who had visited the construction site. He didn't appear intoxicated but was very committed to his description of the prior evening.

"Maybe it was a Banshee," said Butch under his breath. He followed the officers to their squad car and collected his brother. Meanwhile, he kept an eye out for the legendary spirit that warned of death and might snatch you away.

"Well, we're all a bit anxious over this old - what – roundhouse?" said Tim. He pulled the tarp back again and pushed the door open. Then, pulling his iPhone out, he selected its flashlight option and entered the structure.

"Hey – you can't do that. They will not like..." began Julia.
"We've been blessed, and so has it, "said Tim.

Julia paused momentarily, then zipped up her jacket and slung her purse over her shoulder. Tim gave her a thumbs-up and pushed the door open again. Julia turned on her iPhone's flashlight and followed Tim inside. Curiosity and the cats.

It had probably once been a large room with a massive firepit in the centre and logs for seating around the outer edges. Some of the roof had caved in with clay shoving through into the main room. It did indeed look like some bracing might be needed. However, it was a solid structure of cedar posts with willow wattle woven between them and daub plastered over it. The roof was thatched with saplings and reeds. There were two large interior posts with painted carvings of people without facial features. The building was shifting noticeably to correct itself.

Julia's light shone on walls following the lines of various paintings, which depicted animals transforming into other animals and even people. Against one wall was a loom with textiles in progress, loom weights, and a spindle whorl nearby. Julia touched the weaving and admired that it was old but intact.

"Julia – check this out," called Tim.

In the centre of the room next to the firepit was a large stump with a quem stone for grinding set in a central crevice and various leather, wood and bone tools around it. Beside that was a huge brass cauldron or cooking pot sitting on a ring of stones, allowing access to a smaller firepit beneath the pot. It was filled with liquid, possibly water. There were carvings all around the sides of the stump and the log benches nearby. The firepits seemed to grab Tim's flashlight beam and began to glow. It was a soft yellow light that flickered like a flame. The water's surface in the cauldron began to bubble, and a cloud of white smoke or steam rose from it. Both were giving off warmth as if they were ablaze.

Julia was transfixed. The flickering of the light was hypnotic true. Yet, the overwhelming feeling of being home, safe and exactly where she belonged held her to the spot. Tim approached the pot and tentatively placed a hand on it. It was cool to the touch.

The steam from the cauldron rose and hovered together with smoke from the firepit. Finally, the firepits glowed more brightly, and the smoke and steam began to take form, alternately flickering and becoming solid as if the wifi reception was a bit off. Eventually, she could make out the form of an older woman holding a bundle on her right shoulder.

"Timothy Leon Mansfield!" said the vision. "I did not raise you to be such a jerk."

Tim stepped back quickly. "Mom?"

"What if someone treated your sister or your wife so inappropriately?" The woman's light flickered and then faded almost completely.

Tim sputtered and then hung his head. His posture was that of a young boy in deep trouble.

"...Or your daughter." The woman became less transparent and her voice more robust. She turned the bundle in her arms to show its occupant - a baby.

Tim sank to his knees and sobbed.

"Grace is here with me, and I will watch over her. The loss of a child is tough on a marriage, Tim. Sara needs you to help her grieve. She doesn't blame you – she blames herself." Julia watched as the baby cooed and responded to the woman.

Tim stood up with a gasp. "What? I'm probably the one with crappy genetics or something!"

The vision shook her head. "She thinks it was something to do with how the pregnancy went and that it was her fault. The reports were inconclusive, meaning **no answer**, not a lack of anything or a misstep by either of you. Grace's life was brief, but make it count for something. You created life through your love for each other. Please let that love carry you forward. Go home to Sara."

Julia stood slack-jawed and frozen to the spot. She saw his mother and heard every word. If he was crazy, so was she. What the actual hell was going on?

"Julia?" The voice changed, and the image flickered in and out. Finally, the smoke and steam took the form of a man's face with a full beard.

Julia squealed in shock and said, "Dad?"

"You are a good soul with a kind heart. Trust your gut. Tim is a good man for the job, but he must make restitution for his behaviour. You know that the solution is an intervention meeting with your staff. Thank you for all you do. Know that it does make a difference to your team."

The image outstretched his arms, and she could smell his aftershave wrap around her, and then he was gone. Tim and Julia slipped out of the structure, replacing the tarp and hurried to Julia's car. Julia tossed her jacket and purse into the backseat, oblivious to the cold. She still felt the warmth of her father's embrace.

Chapter Ten

Ira jogged across the school field to the bench and sat down heavily. He unsnapped the chin strap on his helmet and dropped it between his feet. His breath came in clouds against the chilly autumn air. He leaned forward, resting his elbows on his thighs, sweat dripping from his hair onto the grass.

"Gonna spend the whole game on yer ass, or are you gonna actually play football, Goldie?" bellowed the Coach.

Ira shifted on the bench, easing the throbbing of his right hip and shrugged sheepishly. It was a rough game, football, but he was also too much of a lightweight against a bigger, older team.

"If yer done fixin' yer makeup, maybe you can catch that damn ball and run with it," snarled his coach into the top of his head.

Ira Goldie jumped to his feet and trotted back onto the field, snapping his helmet strap firmly as he ran. He bent over and froze in position, waiting for Marco Da Silva to call the play. The ball flew up and into Marco's hand. Ira ran out a few yards to where he expected Marco to throw the ball. All eyes were on that ball as it flew end over end through the air. Well, not all eyes – Jerry Smythe and Vince Carter were watching Ira. They ran from either side of the field to converge in one united force of annihilation. Jerry and Vince slammed solidly together, with Ira between them, as Ira's hands closed over the football.

Ira had jumped into the air, one with the football, willing it to sail into his grip. He knew the perfect euphoria that comes with athletic success for the moment when man intercepted football. And then he knew the depth of pain and anger as Jerry's helmet crunched into his right ribs and Vince's well-padded shoulder plowed into his left side. Ira held onto the ball despite the impact and the wind being knocked out of him. He managed to keep on his feet for a split second until Larry Anderson slammed into - no through - his legs, bending them at an unnatural angle and knocking everyone to the ground. The sound of bones breaking could be heard in the stands, followed by a shrill scream of pain from Ira, who still clutched the ball to his chest.

"What the hell is this?" exclaimed the Coach. "Goldie, shake it off. Let's go!"

"Have you lost your mind?" countered Miss Sanderby, meeting his aggressive stance. "His leg is broken. He is going to the hospital."

"Mind your own business," growled the Coach. "Go back to dispensing bandaids."

"Stand down, or I'll have you escorted off the field, Coach." The voice of the referee boomed over the others.

Ambulance attendants loaded him on a stretcher, and he was whisked to the hospital. He remembered little of the pain but all of the softness of Miss Sanderby holding his hand.

"Ira, honey, please find another pastime that gives you joy."

The words he'd heard today were similar, and so was the voice. It was a comforting melody of tones that dripped with kindness and concern. He nodded and grunted in response to Henry's monologue for the rest of the shift.

Officer Ira Goldie, a rookie policeman, volunteered at the food bank, was the owner of one cat and was loved by family but no special partner yet. He wished upon all the stars in heaven that he could pursue something that gave him joy.

At the end of their shift, Ira dropped Henry Zajic off at his minivan and parked the squad car. Shortly afterward, he drove his snappy new Toyota back to Meeachan Park. But, again, he felt an uneasiness in his gut—almost an anticipation of disaster.

He parked on a side street near where the fire had been this morning. He got out and locked the car, moving to the truck and opening it. Officer Goldie removed his official jacket and hat. He tucked them neatly in the trunk. Then he pulled off his belt with cuffs, a holstered weapon, and assorted instruments of his profession, placing them next to his jacket. He patted his pockets, removed his badge and then Ira Goldie slammed the trunk hood shut.

He walked briskly across the street and down the sidewalk to the end of the block. His breath puffed in the cold, and he regretted leaving the jacket momentarily. He entered the lobby of an apartment building and buzzed the intercom three times. Finally, the lobby door lock buzzed and clicked. Ira entered and stepped into a waiting elevator.

"Hello, stranger!"

Ira entered and closed the apartment door. The living room looked like a clothing store had blown up. There were hangers of clothing lying across the sofa and piles of folded items on the ottoman. Boxes of boots, shoes and handbags were lined up on the coffee table, and a cluster of hats filled the seat of an armchair.

"I thought you weren't going to come tonight."

Ira followed the voice into the small kitchen and decided his friend was much more organized in this room.

"I decided to find some joy after all," he said to no one in particular because the owner of the other voice had disappeared.

"Oh! I'm so glad," said Ray, emerging from the even smaller bathroom, toothbrush in hand. "You'll have a blast."

The intercom buzzed three times, and Ray slid past Ira to open the lobby door with a press of a button on the wall in the hallway. "That will be Chad and Ronda, now."

Shortly after, two people arrived, both wearing security uniforms. Ray explained that they were coworkers from the company that did arena security and other sites. They had all worked the Drag Queen show last month and had chatted about it over beers afterwards. Several patrons had told Ray and Chad about a bar in town that hosted Drag events and where patrons were encouraged to hang out dressed in drag. The two men had since been there several times and found it very liberating to dress and be in a safe place. Ronda loved drag and had a hoot helping them get ready. So tonight, she'd go with them dressed as well.

"We'll be a foursome, darlings," said Chad, feigning an English falsetto.

Ira had dressed in his mom's clothes as a youth and loved the scent and feel of her silky outfits. He liked the way his legs looked in her heels, too. Eventually, he bought his own as an adult and kept it hidden from his family.   Ira had once dated someone who understood, but she kept borrowing his lingerie. That ended badly, and he'd never shared about himself again until he met Ray.

Ray Shannon was a man's man, as they say. Ray was suited to his profession and was typically masculine with a gruff voice, broad-shouldered build, and no-nonsense presence. He was friendly but not flirtatious, stern but gentle and kindhearted.   He loved wearing a skirt and heels, especially a tight leather skirt and six-inch spike heels.

Ray and Ira met at the arena. Ira worked an arena Officer-On-Site shift, and Ray had asked for backup to assist in settling a fistfight between three patrons. Ira and his partner that night, Officer Candace Shields, attended the scuffle.   Once tempers were eased and things sorted out, Candace escorted the patrons out and waited with them for a cab. Ira and Ray consulted over the paperwork details.   Ray's partner, Ronda, had mentioned that the one female was dressed in an outfit that she wouldn't wear, but Ray would look good in it.   The comment was made quietly but not out of Ira's earshot. Ray caught Ira's brief expression, which said Ira would have worn it too.

Ira called Ray a few days later to follow up on missing information that wasn't germane to a situation that had resolved itself. The two met for coffee and became friends.

Ray had mentioned this new bar to Ira, but the latter was not ready to venture anywhere in drag. However, he did go with them the last time in his usual Canadian tux and found that the venue had a nice feel.

"Appies are ready!" called Ray from the kitchen.

The foursome spent the next hour trying on outfits and building their resolve. Ronda did everyone's makeup, including her own. Ira selected a simple wig with shoulder-length brown hair rather than the more elaborate hairdos of the others. He then practiced walking in several shoes until choosing a pair that was sexy but dance-practical.

"You must be able to twirl all night long in that gorgeous chiffon dress!" said Ronda.

"Oh yeah, but you'll still get blisters," said Chad, balancing gingerly in a pair of stilettos.

"Okay, let's go. I'll pull my car around to the front and pick you girls up there," said Ray, ushering them out the apartment door.

Ira, of the chiffon dress and white platform sandals, wiggled his cute little butt while swinging a lovely white beaded purse on a silver chain strap. Ray handed him a puffy pink ski jacket and pushed him out the door. The dread in his gut was still there, but excitement fluttered around it.

Chapter Eleven

Stella Zajic was a fine woman. She kept a tidy home and had raised two well-behaved young men. Stella was a no-nonsense, honest, straightforward community member, praised for her calm and sensible approach to crisis and complications. So Henry Zajic was surprised to walk into his home and find much excitement in the kitchen.

Stella Zajic had a boy of about ten years old in a tight grip by the scruff of his sweater collar sprawled over her lap. She was drumming the seat of his pants with her best wooden spoon. The boy squirmed and bellowed his displeasure, more at the confinement than at the blows delivered. His face was red and splotched with rage, as was Stella's, noted her husband with growing alarm.

"Here now!" he said, clapping his hands repeatedly. "What the sam-hell is going on in this house?"

Neither his wife nor the boy took any notice of him. It was as if he were invisible. This was entirely too much for a member of the municipal police department *in his own home*!

"Now, see here, Stella! Who is this boy?" he said slightly louder, if a bit piercing, at the end. "STOP, I say. STOP RIGHT NOW!" This last bit came in the booming, full-on cop tone reserved for weapon-drawn encounters. It came up from his toes and took all of his wind.

Stella's hand stopped mid-stroke. The wooden spoon raised high and poised to complete its mission. The boy stopped moving and screaming. Both of them looked at Henry in shock.

The boy came to his senses first and took the opportunity to escape his sweater and Stella's grip, then bolted out the front door as it stood open. Stella looked at the garment in one hand and the spoon in the other. She arose from her chair and put the spoon on the table, absentmindedly folding the shirt and placing it beside the spoon. Then she tucked the chair back in its place at the table.

"Dinner will be ready in about ten minutes."

Officer Henry Zajic picked up his packages from the doorway and closed the front door of his home. He turned the bolt and slid the door chain into its slot. Henry was a precise man, and now he hung his official jacket on precisely the correct hanger in the closet. He placed his uniform hat on the right hook on the closet wall and his weapon in the safe on the highest side shelf. He removed his boots and lined them up on the closet floor against the back wall. Then, turning slowly, he walked through the kitchen and into the living room.

Stella was humming to herself and tending to something in the oven. Several pots boiled happily on the stove.

The living room was brightly appointed with an overstuffed sofa and chairs sharing a yellow and gold floral upholstery. The large teak coffee table was festooned with doilies and a vase of flowers. The drapes were drawn open, and the pink of the setting sun reflected in the mirror over the fireplace. White lace curtains fluttered in a soft breeze. If not for the pile of broken items, some of which sparked in the fire and crackled menacingly, it would have been an inviting moment.

Henry tapped at the broken pottery and shards of glass with a fireplace tool and determined that Stella's treasures had been substantially lost that day. A fluffy pink kitten's head melted in flames, and he recognized that as something from her childhood.

Henry unbuttoned his uniform shirt and sauntered into his bedroom via the ensuite bathroom. As he changed clothes, Henry turned and looked about the room for the old wooden chest that usually housed Stella's treasures. He concluded that she must have moved it into her sewing room. Then, pulling on a sweater, Henry returned to the living room.

The boy must have taken her things, but how did he find them, and what was he doing here in the first place? Henry had enough mysteries to deal with in his daily police work. He preferred his home life to be quiet and expected it to conform to habitual standards of conduct. In contrast, Henry found change and spontaneity taxing and disturbing. He swept the remainder of the pile into the fireplace with another tool, then, picking up his newspaper, settled himself in his chair.

Stella finished setting the table and began scooping food from the pots into bowls. It would have been easier and more efficient to plate the meal for each of them, but Henry liked seeing all the options and determining whether he'd save some of the meal for lunch at work the next day. He would instruct her on what was to be packed, precisely how much and in which plastic containers. Henry did not like surprises, even lovely ones, as she found out early in their marriage when she had included a note expressing her love for him. He was mortified by the paper touching his packaged meal. Not the food but the container it was in. He was also upset that one of his co-workers might have seen the note and known his private business.

Stella did not express her love to Henry again, but she thanked him for feeding and housing her every evening and had trained their two children to do so. Tommy and Barry were all grown and living in far-off cities. They had exciting lives full of adventures that didn't meet their father's approval or understanding. However, Stella did understand and was pleased for them.

Supper was displayed in various serving dishes on the dining room table. Henry seated himself at his usual place as she poured two glasses of ice water. Stella put the drinks on the table and slid into her seat.

"How was your day?" asked Henry, examining his knife as it cut into a pork chop.

"Oh, the usual. Lunch with Sheila and Roseanne at Moxie Grill after a morning of sorting donations at the Thrift Shop," replied Stella.

"They still have those Bellinis, you ladies like?" Henry's voice was quiet, and he watched her under his eyelashes. Stella bristled, sighed and relaxed.

"No. I am not intoxicated." Stella straightened her back and had an offended posture but said no more.

Henry put down his cutlery, folded his arms and sat back in his seat. He looked very closely at his wife. Stella picked up the saltshaker and caressed the lines of its design thoughtfully.

The pepper shaker was missing, noted the policeman. These were part of a wedding present set, he recalled.

"I came home to find that boy going through the garbage bin in the carport. He startled me when I drove in," began Stella. "I realized that he was cold and hungry. He said he was homeless and lived with his mother in the park."

"Ah," said Henry. He leaned across the table and took Stella's other hand. She pulled it away.

"So I thought it would be okay to bring him in and feed him – and wow, could he eat! So cute to see him brighten up over that cake that was left over from Sunday, too." Stella smiled, remembering. "Then I went into the back storage room to see if I had any of Tommy or Barry's clothes left. I didn't donate them all, in case...."

"They've only been gone a few years. Reasonable to think they may at least visit," said Henry, nodding but puzzled at her avoiding touch. That was usually important to Stella.

Stella nodded. "The boy – Paul, his name is – took the opportunity to ransack our bedroom for valuables. When he could only find things too heavy – like the TV – or of no value, like my trunk of junk – he got angry and smashed everything."

"Ah. Okay. I see your need to correct Paul's behaviour, but you lost your temper. So unlike you, Stella," noted the husband. "What else is going on?"

"We drove by Meeachan Park today. Roseanne said the news was talking about a fire in the homeless camp." The wife stopped and looked her husband right in the eye. "Lots of people mulling about the fire area. Investigating. She drove to the petting zoo parking area to turn around as there was nowhere to park along the street near the fire."

"When was this?" Henry fidgeted with his fork.

"About the time you came out of that construction site with that woman," she said. "I've seen her at department family events but don't remember her name. Lovely long brown hair and usually wearing something very tight and pink."

"Who? What?" said Henry. "I was there, yes. Ira and I were investigating the fire scene. We'd found some tracks...."

"It was NOT, Ira Goldie," Stella said, red-faced and furious. "I'm confident I could tell the difference between a man in a police uniform and a woman in a bright pink down-filled ski jacket and long brown hair.

"No. Stella – something bizarre happened...they uncovered something in the construction site," said Henry.

"Uh-huh. I suppose you'll say that you and Ira found each other and true love or something now, will you?"

"No. No...there was a building, and the door had wooden carvings. There was a glowing light and a...force...field." He paused, realizing the absurdity of his statements. "And we heard voices."

"And that made Ira turn into a woman so he could hug and kiss you in the parking lot? Did the voices tell you your wife will be pissed with you now?" asked Stella. Her body was shaking with rage. Henry had never seen her so angry.

"No, a voice told me I'm an asshole and have neglected my wonderful wife. Suggested that I might take an early vacation and finally take you to Maui." Henry pulled a brochure from his back pocket and slid it across the table. "I need to pay more attention to appreciating you and stop being afraid to tell you how much I love you."

"Why would you be afraid?" asked Stella, momentarily distracted.

"People that I love leave me. My parents, my siblings...my children," he said.

"Oh, Henry. I'm afraid to tell you I love you because you push me away."

Henry stood up, moved quickly to his wife, and pulled her into his arms. He hugged her tightly, and they kissed.

"What did the voices say to Ira?" said Stella after a few minutes.

"They told him to find joy," he said.

"Maybe that was her name," mumbled Stella.

Henry and Stella resumed their meal and chatted about current events. Stella watched her husband closely and believed none of his stories. She and her friends had discussed their marriages at length over the years, and Stella was not as naïve as her husband thought. She knew full well that he had affairs but had aged and slowed down lately. The woman in the park had turned and waved at Stella. She saw her face clearly and recognized her as one of the office staff at the police department when she was working with the Cops for Cancer fundraising events in Barry's high school. That had to be ten years ago.

Henry watched his wife closely and did not for one minute believe that he was absolved. Her description of the women was a dead ringer for Joy Eversen, who had worked in accounting at the station. They'd had an affair, and Henry was smitten like a schoolboy with the young woman. He paused, lost for a moment by the memory of her scent, the softness of her lips and the firm perkiness of her breasts. But then the memory shifted to the day she told him she was pregnant and their argument. Abruptly, she left her job, the city and him: she wanted nothing further to do with him. He was heartbroken. That was ten or eleven years ago.

Brown hair. He was rummaging through the bedroom and looking for – what?

Henry's eyes met Stella's eyes, which were filled with tears. Paul. He was similar in build to his sons at the same age and just as hot-tempered.

Could it be?

They finished their meal in silence, separated by thoughts and weary of the effort to resolve anything more. Finally, Stella cleared the table and cleaned up the kitchen. Henry returned to his chair and newspaper in the living room.

Then, on page D9 in the Lifestyle Section of the Times Colonist newspaper, under the byline of Delia Ismat-Campbell, was the headline: *Homeless Family Victims of Arson*. The article told of a young family, husband, wife and two children who were homeless and camping in Meeachan Park. They had been evicted from their home as the landlord wanted to do renovations. The husband had lost his job in the pandemic, and the wife had been working remotely. The family could not find another place to live in a tight vacancy market and had stayed in a motel for the duration of the renovations, using up their savings. Finally, the landlord allowed them to apply for their old suite but had doubled the rent. The wife had been unable to keep her job as the office was remote workers only, and they could no longer afford the motel and its WiFi. Amid all this and now finding themselves homeless, pranksters had decided to set fires in the homeless encampment. The family, Joy, James, Paul and Nicole, were one of several families who had been subjected to hate and violence in this arson attack. What was the city going to do about it? Henry looked at the photo closely. Paul was definitely related to him.

Henry folded the paper such that the article was entirely in sight. Then, he braced himself and went into the kitchen. Of course, Stella would not be happy, but he had to regain her trust.

Chapter Twelve

Lisa and her co-worker, Maureen Gallagher, sipped their tea in the lunchroom of their government office building. They discussed the social committee's project of collecting hats, mitts, socks and toiletry items for the homeless shelter. A Christmas season project usually, but since homelessness was increasing in the city and the shelters seemed to need more help than an annual drive would achieve, their division had decided to make it an ongoing thing.

"I wonder if we should be dropping donations off to the encampments too, or instead. It seems like there is no room for many people, and if they aren't getting into the shelter, they won't be receiving any of these items," said Lisa.

"Or food, probably." Be nice to take coffee and sandwiches or something out to the Meechan Park encampments. I heard that the city has decided to let them alone until spring. Not like many tourists tramp through the park in this wet weather," Maureen commented.

"I think some non-profit group already does that, but we can mention it at the next social committee meeting," said Lisa.

Maureen and most of the staff in this division were young and full of ideas for bringing inclusivity and diversity to the work of the ministry. It was exciting and tiring for Lisa to listen to their discussions and policy development. She'd been in government a long time and had seen the best and brightest lose their shine when the reality of the layers of bureaucracy and influence complicated and sometimes blocked attaining even the most minor improvements.   Desperate times called for quicker action or some action. A business case for the economic feasibility had to be drawn up and weighed against the needs of the destitute.   Even then, developing a policy was less complicated than implementing it.

Lisa glanced at her watch and noted that Karl's chemo treatment would be done shortly. He and Peter would pick her up afterwards. She returned to her workspace and sorted through some packages from the storage facility. Two files were requested by the Freedom of Information team and had a higher priority.

The first file was background information regarding a young boy who had run away from a local foster home. Lisa glanced through the file to ensure it was correct. She noted that the child had spent his fourteen years, rather sadly, moving through several foster homes interspersed with returns to his mother.   She emailed the social worker and printed the email to accompany the file. The file was repackaged and set aside for the moment.

The second file was a slim folder that contained little more than the adoption order granted by the Supreme Court for a private international adoption. There was very little information about the child adopted beyond a summary from the lawyer indicating that the adoptive parents had been visiting family in Saudi Arabia and had found a little girl of about two years of age in an orphanage. The couple had been alerted to the child by a relative who worked in the orphanage and had told them that the other children did not accept this child with white blonde hair and brilliant blue eyes despite her brown skin. The couple, a mix of Middle Eastern and European heritages, swooped the child away immediately.   Having circumvented the international screening procedures for potential adoptive parents by choosing the child first and applying to adopt almost as an afterthought, they found returning home to Canada with the child complicated. The lawyer spoke powerfully of the urgency of taking the child out of a racially discriminating and possibly dangerous situation. Lisa could well imagine the anxiety the parents had felt. Unfortunately for the child, now looking for information on her birth family, there was nothing useful in the file. Lisa packaged the file and delivered both parcels to the main desk.

Looking out the window, Lisa noted that dark clouds were threatening rain. An old man was pushing a shopping cart along the far side of the street below. At the same time, other pedestrians walked around him, their posture expressing agitation or apathy for the most part. He wasn't asking for handouts, merely walking, but she hoped her response would have been more empathetic. Maybe she'd have stopped him and asked if he wanted some cash or the granola bar in her purse. Well, no. She didn't carry cash anymore specifically to avoid such interactions, so that was unrealistic, if not contradictory. *Enough snarky thoughts, Judge Lisa. Back to work.*

Chapter Thirteen

Below on the street, Jacob pulled his shopping cart into a bus shelter and sat on the bench. His old bones ached in the damp cold. It would be nightfall soon, so he better hustle to his spot under that big tree and set up camp. He hadn't seen Sam for a few days and was worried about the kid. These young ones were not very smart about life on the streets. Sam was learning, in any case. Jacob had found a few tarps and had a makeshift cover that would do for now. The stolen tent would be hard to replace.

"F'kin' aholes," he grunted, remembering the theft of his belongings.

Jacob pushed his cart along the street and hummed an old song to himself. Finally, the sidewalk ended at an abutting road, and Jacob stopped briefly to look both ways for traffic. Then, he pulled his cart over the curb and pushed it to the opposite corner. Just as the old man arrived at the curb and prepared to lift the shopping cart again, a small car sped towards him, slowed to wait, and then honked at him. Jacob hurried to mount the curb, and the vehicle roared past him, turning the corner onto the next side street. Jacob shook one finger in salute to the blazing red letter L displayed on the car's rear window, indicating a novice driver.

"Tabernak!" he cursed. "F'kin' crazee drivers."

Jacob continued down the sidewalk to a paved bike path and into the park. It would be shorter to cut across the grass by the fountain, but pushing the cart through grass, mainly snow-covered or wet grass, was too much for his old arms these days. Jacob made his way deep into the park to a spot where the paved path diverted toward the pond. He braced himself and pushed shopping cart wheels onto the grass, expecting some difficulty. Still, the ground was firm, and he moved with a reduced speed but comfortably. He placed his mobile life's treasures against one end of a park bench.

It was secured to a cement pad and surrounded by a group of trees, with the largest one providing a lovely natural roof for him. He spread a tarp over the bench and then a sleeping bag on its seat.

Next, Jacob rummaged in his cart and found two blankets. He draped another much bigger tarp over the whole thing, including the cart. Then, he secured one end of the second tarp with bungee cords to the base of his shopping cart and rolled back the covering so that he could sit on the sleeping bag. Finally, Jacob poked around in his cart and found a can of beans, the remains of some day-old pastries, and a can opener. He opened the can of beans and tucked the opener away. Jacob sat down heavily, weary, almost too exhausted to eat.

"Ah, but deez cakes will be sad if I doan eat dem up." He said with a raspy cackle, pulling a tablespoon out of a pocket and rubbing it with the corner of his shirt.

Jacob found that the first few spoonfuls of beans soothed his dry throat and caused his sleeping belly to roar to life. He cleaned out the can quickly, scraping the sauce from the sides. He licked the spoon clean and tucked it back in his pocket. Sitting back against the bench, Jacob looked out across the park. He watched other people with packs and wire carts heading across the lawns and pathways to various parts of the park. The evening residents were checking in to nature's hotel.

Night fell fast in the winter, but now, in the early spring, there was more time between dust and total darkness. Enough time to ensure his day-old cakes felt appreciated and his hunger was abated.

He climbed into the sleeping bag and tucked the blankets over himself. Finally, he pulled the tarp down over all of this and secured it to the underside of the park bench with another bungee cord. Snuggled in as best he could, Jacob listened to the rustle of the trees and voices somewhere far off. He whispered the prayers that ended every day for him since he was a young boy.

The nuns had made them kneel on the cold floor and recite prayers out loud. He'd get a smack on his head if he forgot a word or was too slow. He remembered the nuns well: their faces, voices, and the feel of the wooden ruler on his fingers. Often, they spoke of being good to get into heaven or not doing as he was told and going to hell. He imagined that God or some assistant angel had kept track of his sins on an abacus like the nuns had taught him to use when counting inventory in the school's basement storage. He'd pushed the wooden beads along its wires - one bead for each item. Although he liked the squeak as the bead moved, controlling that sound and irritating Sister Maria Theresa was a tiny moment of pleasure.

Jacob drained the last drops from a bottle of wine wrapped in a crumpled paper bag. He licked the mouth of the bottle and sucked the taste of wine from the spills on the bag. Then he snuggled it back under his coat and drew warmth from its presence.

No, counting his sins would need something else. It would be better to use a set of scales and weigh his bad decisions against his intent to be a good boy, a fine man, a loving father, and a loyal friend. Instead, his best friend had been whatever booze was available or stolen, and he had found no peace since that first sip.

He had not kept his word to his wife and had deserted his family. Jacob's eyes watered, and he coughed with sobs. He missed his family and wondered what had happened to Monique and the kids. A boy and a girl. He couldn't face them when he'd lost his last position for being drunk on the job again. That was so many years ago, but the pain of disappointing them was still fresh. They deserved better than him.

He'd been drowning in his misery for decades and felt that his life on the street was a way to find restitution. He had become the friend and mentor of the newest folks and helped them survive. He had learned much that he was happy to share and never judged anyone. How could he – no one could be a worse failure than he was. Jacob wiped his face with his shirt and settled in for the night.

Chapter Fourteen

"Hey, Baby," Carmen whispered, smiling at the image in the bathroom mirror. "What truck hit you?"

Carmen Sam leaned closer and examined the bags under their eyes and dark roots clashing against the remnants of a bleached mop of hair. They winced as the drilling of a hangover headache peaked for a moment. Carmen or Sam, as they preferred, splashed cold water on their face and patted a dampened cloth to the nape of their neck. Yet again, they wished for a house with a jacuzzi to ease their aching body, but they would have to work at something more profitable than flipping cheeseburgers to afford any housing.

Tucking everything into two backpacks, they plopped an official cap on their head and teased out a few pieces of hair. Then, buttoning up a uniform shirt, they gave themself one last glance.

"Hey, Baby, " they said with a wink. "Want fries with that?" Sam had met a man in the Soup Kitchen line who knew someone hiring at a burger place. The man and several others were squatting in the garage next door to the restaurant with the permission of the restaurant owner. Sam had slept on a stack of wood skids in the back and on their own. The others slept together and played together based on what Sam had heard at night. Three days of work so far, and Sam liked it. No one bothered them at night—no sleazy sales manager pawing them during the day, just cleaning tables and prepping food for the cooks. Not bad.

Sam missed seeing old Jacob daily. He hadn't been in his usual haunts, but Sam could have just been off on timing with this new working schedule. Backpacks are stored in a storage room, and Sam is set to chop veggies and listen to the chatter in the kitchen. The restaurant owner paid out wages and tips daily to Sam and two others who slept next door. Settling under the table was common in seasonal work and for those with identification missing. Sam would soon have enough cash to bring Jacob some food and wine – perhaps a thrift store tent. Sam would also like the old man to stay in the garage but doubted Jacob would agree. Sam completed their kitchen tasks and grabbed a bucket to bus the tables.

The regular clientele of folks sitting for hours during the day, using the internet wifi connection, reading, writing, or gossiping was changing over to the dinner crowd. Yet, Sam could recognize familiar faces and habitual orders even just a few days in. The dinner crowd had its regulars, too, they'd been told.

* * *

In the far corner, Delia slid onto the bench seat in her favourite booth after draping her coat over her things on the other bench seat. She sipped from a steamy cup, and the foam of a chai latte tickled her nose. She sighed contentedly. Today had been a long, rough day of people-ing in the office, but Delia always found some rest and grounding here. She curled up the edges of the menu, not being tempted by any of the offerings.

The restaurant had a steady stream of customers. Some lingered briefly to eat quickly and sip some warmth before going back out into the cold. Others, like herself, found reprieve and peace in the venue's ambiance. And still, others took their purchases and immediately left. They were anxious to get as far on their way as possible before the weather worsened.

The sound system of the restaurant played a continuous stream of mellow music. It was not as bad as elevator music and even a bit bouncy sometimes. Delia's right hand tapped out the beat of one such song. She examined her fingers, wagging up and down and frowned at their mutiny.

Difficult to commit to a grumpy "untouchable" persona if one's body feels the need to be moved by music. Delia aspired to be allusive and unapproachable. It suited her opinion of the world in general and local people in particular.

Glen noted the finger tapping in combination with the frowning facial features. Another stuck-up twat, he thought. His opinion of the world, in general, and specifically of females, was not far from Delia's thoughts. However, she, at least, allowed that women had good reason to be bitchy, with male behaviour being such an inspiration.

Clare tugged on Glen's sleeve without succeeding in her attempt to get her dad to buy her another drink or, better – some food. She would like to eat if he was determined to sit here and avoid a storm he thought was coming. Her visits with her dad usually were lots of fun. They would do stuff together or watch television and talk during commercials. Nothing big, although once in a while, there was a road trip and camping.

Lately, he had spent more time in these moods when he only wanted to think, and she would play video games on his computer. It was like he was lost in sadness and forgot about everything. Seeing him like that made her sad, and she would cry when he was out of the room.

He had dated a few women since he and Clare's mom split up, but the last one had been around the longest. Louisa didn't move in, but her dad said he wanted to marry her, and they'd move to another apartment Louisa liked better. Clare enjoyed her dad's house better than her mom's place. At her dad's apartment, she had a big area in the living room with a play table, kitchen set, toys, crayons, paper, and books to read. It was always waiting for her to arrive, and she had her own bedroom, too. Clare had to share a bedroom and toys with her younger step-sister at her mom's place. And there was her cat, Oreo, who lived with her dad. Oreo greeted her with purrs and snuggles at the door as if expecting her to arrive and meowed when she left. Often, he would run along the hallways and pounce across the room, chasing her around the apartment. Clare smiled to herself, thinking about that silly cat.

"Is Louisa meeting us here, or are we going home for dinner?"

Glen stiffened visibly at 'Louisa' and turned to smile at Clare. "Louisa is gone," he said. "Just you, me and Oreo for now."

"Oh," she said, examining her hands closely.

"Don't be sad. She loves you but moved to Vancouver for a new job." Glen lovingly watched his daughter. His heart melted, and he wanted to snuggle her forever. He daily found something new to amaze him about this kid. His kid.

"I have to pee," she said and went to the washroom. He watched her walk to the back of the room. She stopped to speak to that woman who was sulking in the corner. The woman warmed to the conversation and appeared to be comparing shirts. Glen was anxious about the interaction, as crime rates highlighted his worldview. He approached them casually.

"Look, Daddy!" Clare said, pointing to the woman. Delia stretched her shirt out to offer a better display of the design. Glen saw that it matched the shirt Clare wore under her now unzipped jacket.

"We match!" they said in unison. Clare giggled with Delia, whose smile was genuine and kind. Clare's shirt was an original design created by Glen's mother for her granddaughter. While she had made several of the same designs over the years, he knew they weren't publicly available.

"Mine was handmade by my mother's friend," said Delia.

"My gramma made mine," said Clare.

"Mine, too," said Glen, unzipping his jacket and displaying his shirt.

"Your gramma? Sandy?"

"Yes. Sandy Whitworth," he said. "I'm Glen Whitworth; this is my daughter Clare."

"I'm Delia Ismat-Campbell, " she said. "That is odd. I was just thinking about Sandy this morning. I miss her so much. So I decided to wear this shirt and feel closer to her."

"You should call her and visit, " said Clare, nodding sagely. "Gramma loves having people visit, but only I can sleep over." The latter was said with arms crossed over her chest and a stern stare—no negotiations on that last point.

"Oh, I don't know about that. Sandy would likely be disappointed in me. She saw some good things in me and made me want to be the best I could be, but I never followed through on it." Delia paused and traced the lip of her latte cup with one finger. "I made quite a mess of things, in point of fact."

Glen sat across from Delia and pulled Clare into his lap. "My mother died when I was a young boy. Sandy kept an eye on me and visited me regularly as I moved around to various foster homes. She wanted to adopt me, but my father refused. Child Services kept sending me back to him. He and my stepmother beat me often, fed me very little and often locked me out to sleep on the back porch. The neighbours would complain, the cops would come by, or he'd go to jail, and she'd drop me off at the welfare office. Sooner or later, I'd be back in another foster home. Sandy would find me, drop by with clothes and shoes, or take me on an outing. She taught me everything from table manners to French verb tenses. She believed in me and told me I could do anything I set my mind on. She taught me to believe in myself. I screwed up, but she was there to help me repair my mistakes and learn from them."

"That sounds like Sandy," said Delia. "She helped arrange my adoption and remained close to my adoptive mother until she passed five years ago. I spent hours learning about my birth heritage when Sandy visited our home. She always had me reading some new book or article about my birth parents' homeland. My mother said Sandy knew more about Saudi than my father did, and he had no interest in teaching me. Perhaps Sandy would understand that I tried but failed the final exam."

"Cryptic. I love a mystery, and so does my mother," said Glen. He turned aside and poked at his phone. "Hey, Mom. What's for dinner?"

"Gramma! I want s'ketti and meat bulbs," said Clare into her dad's ear.

Delia glanced at her phone to see an email alert notification: RelativeDNA – Results posted to your account. "Hmm, a visit with Sandy seems like a terrific idea."

Chapter Fifteen

Peter was not particularly pleased with the plans for the evening. While he had worked several shifts at the arena and liked the Guest Services work, he hadn't finished his training. In addition, he was a bit uncomfortable filling a security position, especially at a different venue and overnight.

Years before, he had done an overnight security shift as a favour for a close friend of his now ex-wife. The friend worked for a local radio station with an annual concert for children in the parklands around St. Margaret's Academy. The radio station had set up a stage on the main lawn of the former convent, which had been repurposed as an alternative school and some government offices. Peter was to park his car within sight of the stage and keep an eye on it to discourage vandalism overnight. The concert would run for most of the next day.

He had been there for several hours and had done two tours around the stage area when he thought he heard a baby crying. Peter grabbed his flashlight and walked around but saw nothing. He suddenly felt chilly for the balmy summer evening, and the hair at the nape of his neck stood up. He turned to see two nuns walking toward him. They passed by close enough for the one actually to pass through him. He felt a deep sadness and terror all at the same time. Peter booked it for his car and spent the remainder of the night locked inside with no issues staying alert. He did another tour at dawn, but there were no further incidents. He was adamantly opposed to night shifts after that.

Karl had done his share of static security and overnights as well. He was also unimpressed with the plans. The security company with the arena contract also worked with other venues around the city. The Friends of Meeachan Park had arranged with the company to have one security guard in their private vehicle parked in the petting zoo lot and observing the construction site. The idea was to dissuade vandalism but not to have interactions with perpetrators. The guard was to call the police if anything unmanageable occurred. Karl's boss had asked that he attend the site as guards assigned to work the site refused to return. The company had difficulty finding a team, and the activity reports during these shifts were strange. The boss wanted his most experienced supervisor to handle the problem, and they had run out of trained staff. Trainees are required to do one shift with a qualified person mentoring. Peter was offered the training shift, and Karl would mentor him.

The two men arrived at the park loaded up with snacks and coffee. The day shift guard reported nothing of concern except that there seemed to be many more animals in the park than was usually the case. Lots of deer and raccoons, and he thought he'd seen a family of marmots amongst the usual rabbits and squirrels. Birds, too- an odd number of birds you'd think would still be down south.

Karl read through the site notes and discovered that people were allowed to camp anywhere in the park, so the guards had not prevented them from camping in the construction area as long as they left the structure alone. He had noticed several tents in what looked more like a meadow in a gully than a construction site. The mud covered lush grass, undergrowth and hundreds of blue flowers. He didn't recall the tree line being so close to the parking lot, but it hugged the structure.

"It says here that homeless people have been pitching their tents near that structure and packing up in the morning without incident. "

"That's good, so we don't have to make them move."

"No. The cops said to leave them be if they stay out of the roundhouse."

More people came, and the area filled up, but a wide berth was given to the roundhouse. There had been some sightings of wolves and a cougar in the northern part of the park. Word spread, and the vulnerable felt even more vulnerable. Some people harvested the flowers and appeared to eat the bulbous roots. There was drumming and singing.

They are getting what they need here - a safe place to rest. Karl watched for fires to be lit as darkness settled, but the roundhouse began to glow instead. He had not seen anyone enter it.

"I'm going to check that out, " said Karl, opening his car door.

"Want me to come too?" asked Peter, remembering the nuns.

"Yeah."

The two men circled the tent city and spoke to a few people. Then, as they approached the building, a man waved them over to himself.

"Don't try and go in there. It won't let you," he said.

"Well, someone is in there. It's all lit up, " said Karl.

"No. No. It does that itself," said a woman with him.

Peter took a deep breath and pushed the door open. A blast of warm air whooshed past him, and the light dimmed. He heard a voice near him and inside his head simultaneously. *"Know your truth and stand up for your people."*

He stepped on something and bent to pick it up. Peter had been raised as a white child, and minimal mention was made of his Metis heritage; however, he knew a Metis sash in all its red patterned beauty when he saw one. He stepped away from the door and held the garment, warm and smelling of a fruity smoke.

Karl watched this with fascination. He tried to step through the doorway and found himself in darkness. The beam of his flashlight showed him a small vestibule with a table and a box sitting on it. He saw that the box had a keyhole in front. He was reminded instantly of the key he'd found at the bus stop. He felt his pockets instinctively and then recalled that the key was at home on his dresser.

"Not the one for this lock; that would be disturbing," he said, and then, "oh."

Karl pulled the metal key out of his jacket pocket and looked at it. Then, hesitantly, he inserted the key into the keyhole and turned.

Click.

Karl lifted the box lid and stepped back as it flopped back on the hinges. And a hand appeared – old and wrinkled with jagged unkempt fingernails. A sudden urge to hum the theme from *The Addams Family* and snap his fingers twice made him giggle. The amusement caught in his throat as he saw the hand was attached to an arm bare and hairless. The hand moved toward him, and despite his instant reaction to pull away, it pushed inside his abdomen fully to the elbow. Karl felt no pain save a weird sense of being rummaged like a suitcase. Then, the hand pulled out, clutching a Dungeness crab. He saw its back feet wriggling and the two front claws snapping in the air. The hand pulled back into the box, the lid slammed shut, and he was shoved out of the doorway.

"Are ya all right, man?" said the man who had warned them earlier, watching him with concern.

Karl looked down and felt for wounds on his belly. Then he looked around and saw several people staying in the tents, standing near and watching. Peter stood by, holding the red sash he'd found.

"Yeah. I think you are correct. This building doesn't want visitors. Best to stay away." Karl closed the roundhouse door and resumed his tour with Peter.

Later, back in the van, the two men spoke about the tent city and the evening tasks but not about their encounter with the roundhouse. Not until Lisa called to check in with them and advise that she was home from work. Karl and Peter told Lisa about the strange things they had seen and heard. Lisa was interested and asked many questions. She offered that the Metis sash, while bizarre in being there, at least made some sense to Peter. Karl's experience did not – even with the added remembrance of Karl's encounter with the woman at the bus stop and having the exact key for the box in his pocket.

Then, they discussed the next few days of activities and organizing rides when Karl noted that he would have his last chemo treatment this week. Lisa wanted to be available to attend and take a video of him ringing the bell. Karl's chemotherapy treatment schedule was nearly complete. The BC Cancer Clinic had a custom of having the patient ring a brass dinner bell to advise that sessions had been completed. Then, staff would gather and applaud.

"Oh, that's creepy," said Lisa. "I'm reading the astrology column in the paper," she continued. "A crab is the symbol for the sign of Cancer."

Peter and Karl looked at each other and then at the roundhouse as it glowed softly.

Chapter Sixteen

"Dinner was lovely," said Delia, patting a full tummy.

"I've got to get Clare off to bed, Mom, but thank you so much for feeding us on such short notice," said Glen. He gathered his and Clare's things. Clare gave her gramma a big hug and shared kisses with the older woman.

"Must have your dose of s'ketti after all," she said, kissing the child's head.

Delia prepared to leave but paused and said, "Could I hang back for a few moments and chat with you, Sandy – do you mind?"

"Oh, course, Delia. It is early yet," responded Sandy.

Glen nodded, kissed Sandy and directed Clare out the front door. He looked back and gave a *call-me* gesture, to which Delia laughed and nodded.

"What is on your mind, dear."

Delia recounted her recent trip to Saudi Arabia and fruitless search for details of her birth family. She told Sandy that the enquiries she had made to her provincial government and the Saudi embassy had directed her to the orphanage and regional records. Failing to get answers following that route, she finally did a DNA test with *RelativeDNA* to see if there were other relatives to be found.

Sandy was dismayed and felt sorry for Delia. Not knowing who you came from could be disturbing and devastating if one let it be. She'd hoped that as Delia aged, she had found her sense of self in her adoptive family. Sandy remembered Delia's adoptive parents being thrilled and loving with their new baby - their only child. Delia's mother took great pains to ensure that customs and traditions of the Saudi heritage shared with Delia's adoptive father were ever present and acknowledged, even as was her Scots heritage. They were open about her adoption and her mixed racial background.

"And what happened with the DNA business?" asked Sandy.

"I have the results, but I haven't looked at them. You were so close to my parents and involved with me as a child - could you be with me as I view them?"

"Absolutely."

Delia pulled out her laptop, went to the *RelativeDNA* website, logged into her account and found a notice entitled *Results*. She clicked on it, and a wealth of information appeared. It outlined her genetic connections to 25 people and several different countries. There was a message from someone in England as well.

"Oh my goodness! You apparently have family all over," said Sandy.

"The message is from someone who shows up in the connections list as two degrees away - a grandparent," muttered Delia, moving between screens.

"That's quite odd. Look at this woman. She shows up as a third or fourth cousin. The face is so familiar," commented Sandy thoughtfully.

"That is Riva - my dad's cousin. We attended her wedding about ten years ago, just before dad died. She lives in Calgary now." Delia stopped and looked at Sandy. "How is she a DNA match when I'm adopted?"

"Read the message," said the older woman, now entirely invested in this process.

"Delia - the analysis suggests that you are a granddaughter of mine. I have two children. My son is gay and has no natural children known to him. My daughter went missing 28 years ago while on vacation with friends. I am contacting you to learn more about your parents and birth. Mavis McLean."

"I think I need that glass of wine now, dear. Did you want one?" asked Sandy.

"Yes. Yes, I do." Delia frequently wished that her parents were still living so that she could share some aspect of her daily life, but at this moment, she was confident that her anger would not have been well received. They, or at least her father, must have known the identity of one of her birth parents. Finding her in a random orphanage was no coincidence. Now, she *needed* the truth.

Dear Mavis - she began...fingers clacking keys in a frenzy.

Chapter Seventeen

In the following weeks, there was much negotiation over the next steps in building the petting zoo's heated barn and the construction site's discovery.

Steve Knoll shuffled papers nervously while watching Mayor Kuku'I Mahina review his report on Meeachan Park. The budget had been blown, but he did his best to keep it in line.

"So, basically, you're telling me that the park has decided to reforest itself, and the rodent population has been unchecked. Your cost-effective solution is to let wolves and goats run loose in a park within city limits. Where tourists wander," she said, looking up from the report.

"That's correct. We spend far too much on wages and supplies, struggling to keep the undergrowth groomed. Letting the goats tend it will help us save on goat food," said Steve.

"And wolves will eat the rodent population," said Kuku'i.

Steve nodded, feeling like a bug under a magnifying glass.

"And the tourists wandering through or the homeless camping out – what of them? Are they on the menu for these wolves?" she asked.

"Wolves avoid human contact and only feed on small animals. Although it's best not to feed the wolves, so we'd post signs," said Steve.

"Ah, and the pets of folks in the homeless camp or some visitor walking their dog through the park?" asked the Mayor.

"What about the goats?" asked Councillor Mira Yuen as she entered the office.

"They'd taste better with ketchup, perhaps," said Councillor Ben Adami with a wink.

"This is not funny, I'm afraid," countered Steve.

"No. It is not funny at all – it's ridiculous!" said the Mayor, rising from her chair. "I am very interested in seeing you present this plan to the council this evening.

The Friends of Meeachan Park, representatives from a local Celtic pagan group, and staff from the Royal Museum and University were to speak that night about the archeological discovery at the park. Naturally, the city council members were excited to hear about the progress. But, historical and spiritual value aside, this was also a terrific tourist draw for the city.

Mayor Mahina and her councillors gathered in the Council Chamber's Anteroom, chatted and collected around the coffee bar. Meanwhile, the city staff moved about the Council Chamber, setting up the session and delivering session materials to the council desk.

The main doors to the Council Chamber opened, and members of the public were ushered to their seats. The group had a nervous buzz, but they spoke in hushed tones.

Once this appeared settled, the side door of the chamber was opened, and the council members entered the room, taking their seats on the riser. Mayor Mahina called the meeting to order with resounded thumps of her gavel. A hush fell over the group, and the city's business followed a precise agenda at the firm hand of the Mayor. Madam Mayor ran a tight ship. She favoured an inclusive vision with input from the citizens of her city, but brevity was crucial for efficient governing in her mind.

Francis Charles spoke, representing the Friends of Meeachan Park, and indicated that an agreement with the museum had been reached regarding construction in the park near the archeological find. The original plan was to build a large barn and education centre to house all the animals and birds during the winter, as the smaller individual structures were inadequate. The expense of boarding them at a farm in the western communities and the relocation trauma for the animals were considerations. Building a new facility was more economical than refurbishing the existing three barns and birdhouses. Given the archaeological discovery on the construction site, they had considered modifications to the plan. However, none met with consensus approval due to the sacred nature of the site. It was then decided that winterizing the existing buildings was the only viable option. Work had begun, and fundraising for the cost overrun was underway.

City Council accepted this report and asked a few questions about the change of plans; more interest was expressed in the roundhouse. Museum staffer Arnold Thomas and Cerrwynn MacDuibh of Ord Brigadeach spoke to those questions and indicated a need to restrict access to the roundhouse. Francis noted that security had been hired to assist with that.

Mr. Knoll presented his report on issues with Meeachan Park maintenance. Unfortunately, his request for permission to introduce wolves and goats to assist was heavily defeated. However, Mr. Knoll noted that the historical spring trek of young cougars into town looking for food might be inspired by excessive rodents and draw them into the park. Wolves would keep them out and solve the problem.

"This is a city park, not a wild safari, Mr. Knoll. So what ARE you thinking?" exclaimed Miranda Lee Sturgeon, Councillor. To which a round of "Hear! Hear!" followed.

Several other items of a housekeeping nature followed on the agenda and were dispensed with quickly. Madam Mayor was pleased.

"Next up. Police Services has a report. Chief Jones?" she said.

"Madam Mayor and Councillors, I have an update on the recent fires in Meeachan Park." He began, coughed, shuffled his papers and coughed again.

"Yes. Go on," said the Mayor, checking her watch.

"The two fires may be related, but we have no confirming evidence. However, the coroner has determined that the individual found in the tent fire was a female, 20-30 years of age, who had born children and was of Northern European descent. The cause of death was possibly smoke inhalation, although the remains were charred from what appears to be spontaneous combustion. There were no fingerprints or dental work to aid identification, but DNA samples were retained for further testing. In addition, carbon dating was done on the body because the coroner noted some anomalies."

"Anomalies?"

"Shape of the skull, long forearms, and a long gash as if from claws. The results of the dating are quite astounding."

The council chamber was filled with rumblings from surprised listeners. Finally, Madam Mayor banged her gavel for quiet.

"Contiune, Chief Jones."

"The woman's bones are approximately 1500 years old."

"What?" cried the Mayor, and then, "Quiet people. I will have order."

There was no order to be had. First, councillors chatted with attendees and attendees with staff. Then, two reporters awoke from their tedious council session trance and bolted out the door to report the news.

Flamekeeper Cerrwynn MacDuibh spoke with Police Chief Jones and discussed the collection of the woman's remains and whether DNA testing samples from older families within the Celtic pagan community might aid identification. Chief Jimmy Charlie of the Esquimalt Xwsepsum Nation joined them and was assured that none of the burial mounds in the north end of the park belonging to the Lekwungen-speaking people, who occupied much of the area for thousands of years before the land was settled by Europeans, had been tampered with and that the remains were not Indigenous.

Professor Charles Bremerton from the University of Victoria requested access for his archaeological team to be extended to include access to the coroner's report and the remains found in the tent fire.

Citing this new information, Susan Ramirez from the Royal Museum of British Columbia requested access to artifacts and reports beyond the scope of documents filed with the council.

The room was filled with discussion and excitement. The Mayor stood up, pounding her gavel to no avail. Then, suddenly, so quietly, a gentle beat could be felt long before it could be heard. One drum. Two drums. Three drums. They were calling the people to stop and listen. The people took their seats, and the drumming ceased. Not a word was spoken, and all eyes were on Cerrwynn MacDuibh.

"I appreciate that this is all fascinating news to everyone. However, these remains are, first and foremost, a lost spirit that has come home and must be cared for by her people. Therefore, any study or access must be done respectfully following our Celtic teachings." She spoke in a firm, quiet voice that was heard clearly across the room and brooked no disagreement.

"I move that we approve both requests for access to the roundhouse site but table requests for any added access pending scheduling approval with the local Ord Brigadeach Flamekeepers," said Ben Adami, ensuring mention in the Council Meeting minutes for his constituents to view.

"Does that work for you, Ms. MacDuibh?" asked the Mayor, seeing her nod her consent, "All in favour?" "Any opposed?" "Carried."

The Council Meeting was concluded shortly after, but the people remained in the corridors of City Hall, huddled in clutches of concerned citizens seeking answers and not without a great sense of foreshadowing.

What would happen next, and did we even want to know the answer?

Chapter Eighteen

The parking lot of the Meeachan Park petting zoo began to fill, and the vehicles' occupants gathered at the edge of the construction site. It was approaching eleven o'clock, and the homeless campers had cleared out of the area. The coven group was respectfully waiting for their priestess.

Cerrwynn MacDuibh and Jasmine O'Donnell arrived together on foot, having travelled by bus to the park. Cerrwynn of the Ord Brigadeach Flamekeepers and Jasmine of Thirteen House Coven were organizing and managing the group assembled to share in worship and the official blessing ceremony for the roundhouse. Cerrwynn's group had been in the roundhouse and guarded Brighid's flame since the site was discovered, but the local coven of diverse pagan traditions was eager to honour the site as well.

As the women and their followers approached the roundhouse, Elise MacLean stepped out of the building with Doreen Dogherty following. These women nodded in greeting to the others and carried large bowls of water, which they placed on tables set outside. Each table had a stack of hand towels and bars of soap. The women formed two lines and began to perform the traditional cleansing ritual to purify themselves. The smoke of juniper branches was passed over each woman as she entered the roundhouse.

Inside, the women seated themselves on the benches that lined the walls of the roundhouse. A fire burned brightly in both firepits. A table at the room's far end was laden with food and drink.

Cerrwynn, Jasmine, Elise and Doreen each stood around the room marking the directions: North, East, West and South. Cerrwynn cast the sacred circle with the point of her athame in a clockwise movement around the walls and invoked the goddess Brighid, chanting prayers and poems. The four women called the corners by inviting the spirits of those directions to share in the sacred circle. The elementals of those directions were recognized and invited to participate. Other group members offered poems, songs, gifts of flowers or herbs and placed offerings near the larger firepit. Red and black candles and crow feathers were placed by the fire for The Morrigan, the triple goddess of prophecy.

Cerrwynn said: "We honour you, Brighid, and seek to draw upon your power of healing and transformation. We recognize you as a goddess of great compassion and strength. We ask that you bring comfort and healing to this place. We ask that you embrace the homeless, the hungry and the sick, transforming them to their highest potential. We ask that you touch the minds and hearts of those who govern this area and help them transform it into the best possible solution for the troubled souls that live here." She tossed herbs, photos, and other items symbolic of the request into the firepit. Blue candles oiled with lavender essential oil were passed out to the other women. Cerrwynn lit her candle by Brighid's firepit and then passed the flame to one of the women. The flame was shared from candle to candle and passed around the group until all held a lit candle.

Members of the Celtic coven began to drum and chant in Gaelic, enacting an ancient shamanic shapeshifting meditation. Jasmine called upon The Morrigan and Anu to attend to the workings of this night and bring the wisdom of prophecy. She lit a large red candle and set it and a handful of crow feathers by the firepit.

Jasmine then joined Elise, sitting near the cauldron filled with bubbling water. They muttered prayers over the water and gazed across its surface, seeking to scry visions. Keeping their eyes relaxed and unfocused, they watched for shapes or patterns to become clear and impressions to whisper to their minds.

Doreen asked the women gathered to share stories from their own lives of healing and transformation to further honour Brighid. The conversation was quiet and mindful of the women scrying, but there were tears of joy and hearts filled with hope.

Suddenly, the sound of wings beating filled the room. The fire dimmed and almost went out.

Jasmine cried out: "I see terrified people running. Children spared but adults badly harmed."

Elise uttered a deep guttural growl and said: " Only fear will motivate change as drastically as is needed here. My daughters, do not come here again until the Summer Solstice."

Cerrwynn urged the group to remain calm. She dismissed the elementals and spirits of the four directions. She advised them to carry out their assigned tasks and return home harming no one on the way. "It is my will, so mote it be." She thanked Brighid, The Morrigan and Anu for their guidance and wisdom. Then she uncast the sacred circle with her athame tip in widdershins motion. "Blessed be," she concluded.

"Blessed be," responded every voice in the room, not quite as one.

Doreen invited the women to share in the traditional feast displayed on the bounteous table. The conversation was limited, and the group dispersed more quickly than anticipated. Many left thinking, '*Be careful what you wish for, lest it come true.*'

Chapter Nineteen

Interest in fires, ancient remains, and strange happenings in the park was short-lived. The news was soon full of groundhog shadows, and the assured arrival of spring contrasted sharply with alerts of old man winter's last dump of snow and miserable cold across the country. Meanwhile, the city of Victoria, favoured by Mother Nature, was decorated with beautiful colours, and the Annual Blossom Count was in full swing. The plight of the homeless was pushed to page 3 and was out of most people's minds.

Spring also brought the animals back to the petting zoo and the Running of the Goats. This occurred every morning and every late afternoon. The resident herd of goats would run from their barn to their exercise stall along a short roadway and then run back later in the day. Visitors would stand along either side of the route, watch and cheer. Once the goats were in the exercise stall, visitors could enter and play with them. This was great fun as they would jump around, head-butt people, and let visitors pet them.

After several years of remote schooling and limited activities, finally, there would be a field trip to the petting zoo and ordinary childhood experiences.

The number 2510 school bus pulled into the petting zoo parking lot and sidled up in the queue with six other buses. All the children, teachers, and parent chaperones were disembarking from the buses and into one big mishmash of bodies. Teachers were calling to their children and organizing them into lines with parents intertwined.

Bembe and Cai Hong bounced out of the bus and ran to line up with their classmates. Bembe's mom, Jalissa, worked at the local hospital, but Cai Hong's mother, Mei Ling, attended and was ready to prod the boys into proper behaviour. Ronica followed and joined up with some other girls from her class. Clare's dad, Glen, also had to work but would be done with his paramedic shift in time to catch the end of the field trip. Clare and her classmates had arrived on an earlier bus and were already waiting at the entrance of the Children's Petting Zoo. Each child had a loonie coin tightly in one hand, as admission was always by donation.

Delia joined the queue with Paul, Nicole, Rosie and Simon, who were all children of the homeless encampment of the recent trashcan fire. Their parents had strong hesitations about Delia taking their children to mix with the school trip bunch and were anxious to have them out of hand. So they gathered across the street from the zoo, watched and waited. First, Delia had the children wave to them, and then she gave each one a loonie.

Soon, hundreds of children were inside the zoo, standing along the main roadway and chatting excitedly.

"Okay, children! Today is the first time the new baby goats have run from their barn to the petting area. The older goats will guide them, but if they run toward you, wave them on that way." Melissa Cartright loved her job at the zoo. Kids, both goat and human, were hilariously entertaining.

Next, a mass of furry bodies jumping up and down ran past them. They stopped, bleated at the humans, and ran toward them or straight down the hill to the petting area. The children laughed and called to the goats. It seemed like a lengthy event, but it was over in a matter of seconds. Then the various class groups moved about the zoo, looking at exhibits of birds, donkeys, ponies, and goats, as well as two large peacocks that strutted and called out loudly. It was all exhilarating for everyone.

Bembie and Cai Hong were, of course, waste deep in jumping baby goats and took turns with them in head-butting practice. Ronica sat on a log in the petting enclosure, petting them as they jumped all over her. Her friends squealed and shrieked, being properly offended by goats chewing their clothing. At one point, Mei Ling had a goat on her head and a fist full of Cai Hong's jacket. Clare stood outside the enclosure, peeking through the log fence, and a goat came up to lick her face.

Paul, Nicole, Rosie and Simon stayed very close to Delia. They all patted the donkey and were awed by the various birds. Paul was a bit brazen with one of the peacocks and fed it some available corn. The bird seemed comfortable around Paul, and the boy said he'd fed the peacocks out in the park before.

Ray Shannon sat at the far end of the parking area, watching the construction site. The homeless encampment had dispersed chiefly, although he could see a few stragglers hanging out across from the zoo. Of course, the parking lot was full of buses and cars, which blocked his view of the zoo, but that wasn't his schtick today, so whatever. He took another sip of his coffee and pondered, taking a stroll around the construction site again.

A light reflection caught Ray's attention, and he noted that the roundhouse door stood ajar and emanated a bright light. The building was now fully recovered and standing in a meadow of tall grass and blue flowers that was no worse for camping, having been done there overnight. Assuming some tomfoolery was afoot, Ray walked around the building.

"Yo. Anybody in there? Speak up now," he called out. There appeared to be no one around. He listened for a moment and thought he heard a mumbled conversation and then a howling. But, no, the howling was from behind him. Ray returned to his car and noticed that the folks hanging about across the street were running toward the zoo entry gate.

"Wolves! Wolves!" They were calling as they ran.

"Lock the gates! Wolves!" They called as they arrived at the gates.

Ray had walked out to see what was going on. Then, he saw it. A massive pack of large grey wolves running through the woods toward the zoo. He made haste for his car, rolled up his window and locked all the doors. Then, Ray wrapped his blanket over his head.

He peeked out and saw that the wolves had surrounded the zoo and were growling at the folks inside. One of the wolves was sniffing around his car but quickly joined the others.

The animals in the zoo were suddenly very interested in getting back into their various barns. The panic quickly infected the children in the zoo as well. Parents attempted to calm them, but Melissa could smell terror on everyone and imagined the wolves could, too. She'd never seen a pack so significant in an urban area. One of two might wander into town or the odd cougar, but not an entire pack. Melissa called Animal Control and left a message. Next, she called 911 and described the problem. While the dispatch voice tried to find referral solutions, the wolves howled louder, and several jumped the fence into the goat enclosure.

The rush of children, parents and goats fleeing the wolves knocked Melissa over and sent her phone into the donkey pen. The wolves inside the enclosure began a multi-course goat feast, causing a frenzy in their pack mates. Finally, wolves jumped against the fencing, and some more made it over.

People and goats were running everywhere. Donkeys and ponies were kicking at the fences, trying to escape. The peacocks had flown out of the area and were watching from the upper limbs of nearby trees.

Ray watched people run from the zoo and try to get into the parked buses. Hungry wolves were still working on the poor goats inside and those few that left the zoo. Some wolves circled a group of children, and a woman was swinging her purse at them. One wolf grabbed the strap of the bag and dragged the woman away. Several wolves joined it, and they feasted on her.

The children with the woman screamed and ran toward Ray's car. He swung a door open, and four got in his back seat. Three others ran past his car and jumped into the construction site.

The wolves seemed to grow in numbers; more circled the buses and drove children and adults away. Some people got into cars, but most were snatched or chased away by the snarling wolves that seemed to be everywhere.

Delia and her charges moved toward the construction site. The kids' parents begged her to run there with them as that spot felt safe lately.

Others followed, and soon, most zoo visitors were at the construction site near the roundhouse. The door opened wider; singing and drumming could be heard. Delia knew that drummers from the local pagan coven would accompany the archaeology team to ask the gods for a blessing on the work. She hoped this was who was drumming and that the goddess would keep the visiting children safe. Many people entered the roundhouse seeking asylum, and its interior light shone like a beacon of hope in the madness of the situation. Delia and Mei Ling stood together, shouting to the others to be calm and see that the wolves were not entering the construction site. Clare suddenly appeared and wrapped herself around Delia's legs.

The 911 operator had called in everyone, including the Mayor. Animal Control, the Police, the Fire Department and several ambulances were dispatched post haste.

The Mayor consulted the Premier, her Park Maintenance Services people and the media. As a result, alerts were sent to keep people out of Meeachan Park. In addition, she called Steve Knoll and had a frank conversation about whether or not he had anything to do with this event to determine the city's liability.

Glen arrived in his ambulance, terrified as to what he'd find. Jalissa's emergency department was alerted to expect injured victims.

As the various levels of defence arrived at the park and began organizing their plan of action, there was a rumble and a roar of thunder. Lightning flashed and struck a centenarian tree, cracking in half right down the middle. The bruhaha silenced the people and stunned the wolves. Then, rain began to pour, and an atmospheric river deluge was noted by meteorologists in the following days.

The wolves scattered with animal control and police in pursuit. Firefighters sorted through the crowd, triaging patients to paramedics who were treated or transported by other ambulances, arriving continuously. Teachers gathered their children and took head counts. Buses were loaded but stood their ground as more police arrived and began to take statements.

Officers Zajic, Donnely and Coleman worked their way through the crowd and urged people to get into their cars or buses and out of the rain but not to leave the scene.

"Henry? Henry?" Officer Zajic turned to see a woman wrapped in a blanket and shivering in the cold rain. Years fell away from his mind, and he saw her young, beautiful face in his memory, somewhat faded in reality, before him.

"Joy?" He walked toward her. She stood with a man, several women and four children. Henry recognized the boy, Paul, and paused momentarily. His eyes met Joy's glance, and she nodded. Although the moment did not invite conversation beyond their statements and getting them to shelter, every detail was engraved on his mind.

Delia watched all this with a reporter's note for detail. Police were sometimes friendly with homeless people but often dismissive. But, in this case, he apparently knew Joy, and his attitude toward her son was almost affectionate. *Nice to see*, she thought.

Mei Ling had organized the others into their bus, and Clare's teacher had gathered her away. Seeing that her guests were in good hands, Delia looked more closely at the roundhouse. The light still shone, but the singing and drumming had stopped. People who had taken refuge were slowly leaving as police processed them. She slid inside and looked around. The interior was beautiful: carved poles and bright paintings on the walls. Turning around in a 360 view, she gasped in awe at each glance. Then, just behind the door, she saw a mural painted in more subdued colours, one of which was a deep brown paint that flaked. The painting was of a woman tending a garden and holding a net of tiny creatures –beetles or something. She held her breath and stretched out a shaking hand to touch it. Then she smelled some flakes of paint. It had a mouldy, earthy scent.

"Well, you wouldn't know the smell of dried blood if you had to know. So what are you thinking?" She said out loud to herself.

"Fifteen seconds remain on your timer," said her phone loudly from her back pocket.

Not sure what timer she'd inadvertently set, but that seemed an excellent prompt to leave the roundhouse. Delia stepped over the threshold and closed the door as she was the last to leave. Then, looking back over her shoulder, she noticed that the roundhouse was in darkness again.

Buses were leaving the area, taking children back to their schools and their parents who had been alerted by the cautionary media messaging. The city had opened temporary warming centres in halls and recreation centres, diverting people from overcrowded shelters and lodging in the park—the police and fire personnel assisting in this relocation venture. A local volunteer hunting group assisted the police and Animal Control officers with the wolves.

Chapter Twenty

Glen and his partner paramedic treated and comforted a steady stream of mildly injured people. Other ambulances arrived and left, transporting the more seriously wounded to the hospital. It appeared the wolves had a taste for human flesh but preferred the adults. He wondered if that was because the children ran faster or the adults had more meat on them.

"Barb, did you radio to base for more supplies?" he asked, finishing with another wolf nip. No stitches were needed, but a series of rabies shots would be prudent when the child's parents could approve the medication at the hospital. The other paramedic nodded and gave him a thumbs-up gesture.

"Hey, Glen – there's a kid – Clare Whitworth – in that bus, closest to the zoo. She can see you and wanted to run over here. So I said I'd tell you that she's with her teacher and fine," said Officer Goldie, consulting his notebook.

"Oh, thank god! Thanks, Ira. Big load off my mind," said Glen.

Officer Goldie chuckled, "She's intent on helping you bandage people."

Barb laughed and said, "That would be Clare, all right."

"Yeah, every doll and stuffed animal has been bandaged and medicated with jelly beans in our house," agreed Glen.

A moment of shared amusement and normalcy gave them a reprieve, and then the tense focus of the situation returned. Unfortunately, no one had time to consider the traumatic impact of these kids being hunted by wolves and seeing their classmates and teachers mauled. Not a standard item in any of their procedure manuals.

The alerts sent out via the provincial alert system, usually reserved for natural disasters, had appeared on every cell phone. It was also picked up by television, radio and social media. Despite the request of the alert to stay out of the park, the traffic around the park was making emergency vehicle access nearly impossible. News media, worried parents, nosy neighbours and countless nervous citizens were gathered against police barriers, seemingly oblivious to the possibility of being eaten by wolves.

"Yes, Madam Mayor. We are doing our best to control the situation. However, wolves are everywhere in the park. For every wolf that is sedated or shot, four more appear. It is the most bizarre thing I have ever seen - right next to the level of stupidity in these people who need to hang about and observe," said Police Chief Jones. His phone vibrated, and he saw that another call was coming through. "I keep waiting to hear Rod Serling's *Twilight Zone* voiceover."

"This is starting to feel more like a Quentin Tarantino movie," said the Mayor, "Keep me up to date as you can, please."

Jones poked at his phone screen and then, "Jones, here. Where are we at with officers from other jurisdictions arriving?"

There was shouting, and some people began running his way. He put a finger in his other ear to continue his call. Jones looked up in time to see several wolves surround a man with a shopping cart. Buddy hadn't heard the alert, perhaps. Likely not trending on the Dumpster Dive social media platform. Several officers had the wolves in their sights, and the attention of some of them was diverted.

"Hey, dere. Git away from me, now," said Jacob. "Dis is not mah day to be yer dinnah!"

He took a rolled-up newspaper and lit it with a lighter. The flame took to the paper quickly, and Jacob waved his torch at the wolves. A hunter with a rifle in hand took down one of the wolves from a distance, and one of the police officers shot another at about the same time. The wolves pulled back, and a second police officer reshot the one wolf as a wounding had only angered it. Finally, the hunter shot a third wolf, but one remained, eyes locked with Jacob. The flame on the paper got too close, and Jacob threw the torch at the wolf, who jumped over it and onto Jacob, knocking the old man to the ground.

Jones had watched all this while retrieving his police league baseball bat from his trunk. The wolf was moving too close to the old man to get a clear shot, but Jones could hit a line drive into the next park on a bad day. So he stepped close and smashed the wolf's head with a resounding crunch. The other officers finished the job as the wolf lay stunned.

Jacob was bitten on his arms, chest, and face but was unwilling to go to the hospital and leave his cart of possessions behind. Jones was negotiating with the man while they waited for paramedics to arrive.

"Jacob! Jacob!" Sam had found their friend at last. They had heard the news of the dangerous situation in the park at the restaurant. Sam had looked everywhere for their friend. Then, finally, one of the women at the Langley Street shelter said that Jacob had been by for pastries and coffee not an hour before. He'd said he was going to the park to find a nice camping spot. One of the other workers had found Jacob a new tent, and he was anxious to figure out how to put it up while still daylight.

Jacob was distressed and in a goodly amount of pain but stubbornly determined and fought off the paramedic's attention. Finally, Sam calmed him down, and his wounds were assessed. Unfortunately, he had burns and deep bites that would need stitches, so Jacob must go to the hospital. Jacob's concern for his possessions was tangible, but he also had no health insurance or money.

Sam was unsure what to do and said that they could take the cart somewhere safe but had limited money for medical bills. A bystander, Louis Riviera, having witnessed the encounter and overhead the conversation, offered to let Sam store the cart in his nearby garage and would call in a few favours to cover Jacob's medical bills. Mr. Rivera had conversed frequently with Jacob over the years in the park neighbourhood and was fond of the older man.

Soon, Jacob was in the emergency triage and awaiting treatment with Sam at his side.

Jalissa assisted Dr. Talon, set up an intervenes line with saline, and made Jacob as comfortable as possible. The emergency team was overloaded with bite victims of all descriptions, stitching, bandaging and medicating systematically. They had many people tended to and released and several people who had been severely wounded and were resting, waiting for further tests. There were now four who had not survived their injuries. Jalissa had seen one of those, and Jacob's bites were much worse. She watched Dr. Talon and listened to his drug orders. Then, she moved to administer medication as instructed. Dr. Talon's intern, Dr. Sousz, began to suture Jacob's wounds. Heart monitor tabs and blood pressure finger monitor were somewhat in the way, but the doctor worked around them, and Jalissa focused on the process.

Jalissa watched the young person who waited just outside the draped cubicle. She saw the tension in their face and could now hear sobs. *Poor ting. Mussi di grandfatha*, she thought.

Chapter Twenty-One

"What do you mean, **they shrunk and then burst into flames**?" said Police Chief Samuel Lloyd Jones. *This Fire Marshall* *missed his calling as a comedian*, he thought. In his 26 years with various police forces and ten years before that in military service, he had never seen a hot mess as this day had become.

"I'm telling you, Jones! I saw it with my own eyes!" exclaimed Logan, punching the steering wheel in front of him with gusto. "The wolf carcasses shrink into that of another animal and then burst into flame. So we have charred remains of squirrels and rabbits – a couple of rats, and this last one is a young buck."

"How is that even possible!" replied Jones.

Logan's mic opened, but the background voices were loud and confused. "Come and see this now! Over here by the Cricket Field – this one is now human."

Moments later, Police Chief Jones, Fire Marshall Logan, Abby Sheer from the Coroners' Office, several hunters, police officers and far too many bystanders stood around the charred remains of a man.

"He was a cougar, you say?" Jones asked.

"Yes, sir. A big old tomcat circled that burned spot where the tent fire was. He was some angry and took on three wolves and then came at Greg and me," said Larry Reilly of the local hunters' group. Greg Kerr, standing near him, nodded emphatically.

"He was not human when we shot him," said Greg.

"You both shot him?" asked Jones.

"It took four rounds to stop him!" chimed the two men in unison.

"I've inspected several of the wolf carcasses around the park, and it takes, on average, a half hour for this transformation to occur. I would venture into the fact that the body needs to cool before the change occurs. Once the change has happened, the combustion is relatively immediate," commented Abby of the Coroner's team.

"On the plus side, the wolves appear to have withdrawn from the park," said Logan.

"Well, that would depend on where they are now," said Jones. He radioed for his officers to tour the park and surrounding city streets to track the movement of the pack.

Confirmations came in that the wolf pack had disappeared as suddenly as they had appeared. Park maintenance trucks collected the animal remains piled throughout the park, but nothing had crossed beyond Meeachan Park borders.

The cougar man's remains were taken to the City Morgue for analysis and possible identification. The Coroner noted some similarities to the tent fire woman – extended forearms and an odd-shaped head. However, no carbon dating was necessary. He was more modern, for cougar man had dental fillings and a surgical pin in his leg. Abby got a partial print from one of his toes and a sample of his DNA.

Days later, Samuel Jones sat at his desk in his office on the second floor of the Victoria Police Services Building. He read one paragraph again and then sat back in his chair, sipping from his

VicPD coffee mug. The cougar man had been identified as Ryan Dean, a 32-year-old man known to police for petty theft and drug trafficking. He was a familiar face outside the shelters and frequented the homeless camps. With plenty of theory and little evidence, the joint departmental investigation determined that young Ryan had set up camp in the park and invited the woman to join him. A fight ensued, causing the fire. Ryan escaped, but the woman did not.

The limited evidence is that the woman presented as a cougar, and Ryan was induced to pose as a cat. Notably, the ruins of the campsite show violence and claw marks to indicate that a large cat fought or mated with another before the fire. The cause of the initial ignition was undetermined, but the source of the fire was the woman's body.

Jones could not wrap his head around a 32-year-old guy and a 1,500-year-old woman getting kinky in a tent in the middle of a public park while turning into mountain cats or pretending so effectively as to leave substantial claw marks.

"I'd like to turn into a Budgie and fly away from this job," he said to the framed photo of his family on the wall.

His desk phone rang, and he sighed deeply before answering, "VicPD. Jones, speaking."

He looked out his window to the street below as he listened to the caller. People were gathering to protest, he was told. The Mayor had called a closed meeting of the stakeholders involved in running Meeachan Park to review events and find solutions. The public was not invited, and by the size of the protest group already surrounding the building – one could assume that some citizens weren't happy to be left out. Fortunately, the rumours had been misdirected, and the meeting was not to be held across the street at City Hall.

Chapter Twenty-Two

Delia yawned and stretched. Sleeping in once in a while was a delight. First, she snagged her mail and Victoria Times Colonist from the floor below her mail slot. Then, pouring that first cup of coffee, she settled into an easy chair with the mail on her lap.

She flicked on the TV, manipulating the channel and volume with the remote control. Local CFAX radio station had a segment with video of the announcers and a ticker tape news bit. She listened to the entertainment news bits and sorted through the mail. Bills, junk mail and flyers, for the most part. One handwritten letter addressed to her with a UK postmark and stamp of the new King William.

Delia examined the stamp and decided the commonwealth was in handsome hands. She gingerly opened the envelope and found a letter in a flamboyant script and two photos. The photos showed a young teenage girl with blonde hair and blue eyes. The smile was familiar, and she knew those eyes. Delia looked at her reflection in the glass cabinet to her right. The same face smiled back at her.

Opening the letter, she began to read the story of Mavis McLean's daughter, Jennifer. A loving child, bright and enthusiastic about life. After Secondary School graduation, she and three other girls took a backpacking tour of Europe. They had studied languages, were well-versed in travel safety, and travelled with a youth group. Mrs. McLean was worried, as mothers do, but Jennifer checked in regularly by phone until she didn't. The youth group tour leader called to advise that Jennifer and her friend, Moira Matthews, had gone shopping together in Budapest but had not returned. The local police would not investigate yet as they had not been missing long enough. The tour leader said that they had to move on in the itinerary. The McLean family and the Matthews family were inseparable for the next two years while the fate of their children remained unknown. Then, Moira's body was found during an Interpol and local police raid on a human trafficking organization in Ankara. Information gleaned from that raid indicated that a shipment of girls had gone to Syria regularly, and an auction was held there for rich tastes.

Delia let the letter slide onto her lap. Her thoughts and emotions spun around her in a whirlwind. She didn't need a DNA test to tell her that Jennifer was her birth mother. So what had happened to her? Delia looked down at her hands and arms and felt a nauseous rumble in her stomach. Budapest to Ankara to somewhere in Syria, and Delia was born in Saudi, And her adoptive cousin Riva is a DNA match? Her adoptive father's family were wealthy oil suppliers. Would they have attended an auction of women? Two of the uncles have several wives, but she had never heard anything about purchasing them. *Well, no. They wouldn't be telling everyone that kind of thing.* She closed her eyes and tried to remember something that was picking at her mind.

At Riva's wedding, Delia's parents had argued in whispers about something to do with Riva's fiancé and a *special treat* Riva's father and uncles were arranging. Delia's father was insisting that it was tradition and he'd had it as well with no ill effects. Delia's mother was incensed to find this out and slapped her father across the face before locking herself in the bathroom. It was one of the few times she'd ever seen her parents argue, and the tension never entirely left their relationship.

"I wonder if the *special treat* was a hooker?" she said, "Or someone stolen, like you." Delia looked at the photos thoughtfully.

Delia pulled her laptop from the coffee table to her lap and lifted the lid. The men may keep the tradition, but a woman like her mother would be asking questions. So, she emailed Riva and asked if she could visit. This would be no email conversation; Delia needed to go to Calgary in person. Next, she drained her coffee mug and set it aside. Picking up the letter, she flipped to the next page and found detailed notes with names and dates outlining the search for Jennifer McLean.

Delia recalled a contact with Global Affairs in Ottawa from a piece she'd done on international adoptions. *Monique LeFleure?* *Yes. She might be a resource on this, too. So* Delia opened a browser and typed in a search for *Human Trafficking, Canadian Govt.* She read through a website called Blue Campaign. She found enough information to clarify that this was still a very active trade, not just in far-off countries – right here in her haven of Canada.

Chapter Twenty-Three

The gymnasium of Victoria Secondary School was always chilly. Arnold Thomas remembered sitting on wooden chairs lined in rows and shivering as a child. The cement floors and walls kept the large room cold even when every seat had a body on it, and lots of children's voices reverberated from the ceiling. Today, the chairs had been arranged in a double-row circle.

"Anyone wanting to speak will have to stand and wait for a staff person with a wireless mic to reach them. I think there are two of them," he said.

"Is that an option?" said the Mayor, "Some have very soft voices. Would a mic stand at the one end work, or is the protocol to speak from your seat?"

"Well, yes, traditionally, one would speak from where one is sitting, but moving to a standing microphone is quite disruptive in this seating arrangement," replied Arnold.

A large map of Meeachan Park was displayed on an easel at one end of the circle. In the centre was a long table with stacks of reference materials, a coffee/tea station and plates of assorted cookies.

The chairs quickly filled with representatives of the local pagan community, City Council, Friends of Meeachan Park and James Bay Neighbourhood Watch. Present also were members of the Victoria Police and Fire Departments and several active poverty outreach groups. Seated at the one end of the table were two city hall administrative staff members, and working in the periphery were technical staff monitoring the audio and recording of the session.

Mayor Kuku'l Mahina stood and waved an arm to garner the group's attention. The room quietened, and all eyes were on her. She sat down again as she spoke:

"I've called us all together today to begin discussions about Meeachan Park and what our next steps might be. I will ask Cerrynn MacDuibh to open this meeting with spiritual clarity, please." One of the city's AV team followed the mayor's direction with the wireless microphone.

Cerrwynn held a seven-foot-long ceremonial speaker's stick adorned with carvings, paintings, and a polished stone lashed to the top but accepted the mic with her free hand. Someone stepped forward and lit a stand of candles at the long table's midpoint. Several attendees sitting in the circle near her sang or played small harps and hand drums, filling the room with song and setting a peaceful mood. The music ended with mournful trumpet blasts of a long-handled Celtic carnyx horn that bore a wolf's head, giving many goosebumps. Cerrwynn gave a brief invocation and blessing on the meeting. Finally, a peaceful hush fell over the room. The mic stand was returned to the Mayor.

"Steven, would you be so kind as to describe the state of repair that we have at the park today," said the Mayor, offering the carved talking stick to him.

"Yes, Madam Mayor," began Steven Knoll, Parks Manager, taking the microphone. "The park is overgrown and in desperate need of substantial maintenance. The Children's Zoo has lost most of the goats, all of the donkeys and a few of the birds. In addition, we have incinerated five truckloads of small rodent remains. However, the destruction to the park and littering resulting from illegal camping has dropped to a minimum."

"Small rodent remains? What happened to the wolves?" asked Alec Murphy, James Bay Neighbourhood Watch Chairman.

"No wolf remains were collected," replied Mr. Knoll.

A mumble passed around the circle.

"I can speak to that," said Police Chief Jones raising his hand. He stood up and accepted the mic from Knoll. He allowed the mic stand to be moved to his spot.

"The wolves that were culled were observed shrinking to the size of small rodents within 30 minutes of the kill, and then they spontaneously combusted. As he mentioned, Mr. Knoll's staff later collected the charred remains," continued Jones. "Three wolves also shrunk to the size of young deer, but no wolf carcasses were found otherwise." He thought: *A cougar or two that turned back into people, but that's another story,* while handing the microphone to a city staffer who put it on the mic stand and moved it to the centre of the circle.

"How is that even possible?" cried several people, and the mumble flew around the room, increasing in tension and volume.

One of the pagan harpists, Siobhan McCrea, nodded to Arnold Thomas, and the latter motioned for the city staffer to bring the mic stand to her. She remained seated, but her voice was strong and clear.

"Ancient Gaelic lore tells us that there will be a time when the old ways of the Lords and Ladies will be needed to heal the land and all creation. Our ancestors built this roundhouse to honour three goddesses who bring transformation and healing. It has returned, and change has begun in the surrounding area. The old legends tell us that the Pucas fill the creature - the squirrel - with their spiritual energy and shapeshift into the best form needed – the wolf. When the squirrel is done needing a wolf's strength, the squirrel absorbs the energy as knowledge and returns to its squirrel form. If the wolf meets with an unexpected death, the energy returns to the squirrel with too much force and the squirrel cannot absorb it. The burning carcasses would be that extra energy."

"That makes about as much sense as anything coming across my desk lately," Steven Knoll muttered.

"Actually, that makes a whole lot of sense given the Coroner's report I just read regarding a man found in the park prancing around dressed as a cougar – so effectively that hunters shot him. His body self-incinerated," said the Mayor.

"Having seen many of these animals revert and implode, I would agree," said Fire Marshall Logan.

"A sight that is not soon forgotten," agreed Cal Perkins of StreetTeam.

"Are the goddesses and spirits protecting the roundhouse?" asked Frances Charles of the Friends of Meeachan Park.

"Yes. The Morrigan can appear as a wolf and howl a battle cry to protect," said Cerrwynn.

"They likely want all those homeless tents gone, too," said Marguerite Van Deuzen of the James Bay Neighbourhood Watch.

Another mumble went around the circle and erupted into excited chatter. Finally, Steven Knoll raised his hands and took the mic.

"Well, actually, the security company guarding the construction site reports that the homeless encampment appears near the structure every afternoon and breaks camp every morning. The campers are respectful and maintain a distance from the roundhouse while telling the guards they feel safe and protected. In addition, they have kept their garbage under control, and the grass immediately recovers after they break camp. Therefore, we have agreed they may camp there overnight if they continue like this," said Knoll.

The Mayor took the microphone and advised that neither wolves nor cougars had been seen in the park or elsewhere in the area for several weeks. She felt that the city had responded to the emergency reasonably but that something more permanent needed to happen. She invited those in attendance to split into small groups and brainstorm with *unlimited budgets and anything possible* project ideas. What are the problems, and what could be the solutions?

The tension of the previous discussion disappeared as chairs scraped the floor and were rearranged. Excited but hushed voices filled the room. Post-It Easel pages were arranged on the gym walls, and markers were given to each group.

Notes began to appear around the room -
What are the limitations on development with the park trust?
What are the needs of those who use the park – neighbours,
visitors, or the homeless?
Warming centres
First Aid Clinic Access
Food insecurity
Mental Health Services Access
Addictions – treatment, safe use sites
Housing, temporary or permanent
Transition housing – domestic abuse
Problems with garbage and crime in encampments
Reassess clearing of underbrush - cost vs fire safety of leaving
it to grow.
Use of the roundhouse for ceremonies only? It could be a
profitable tourist attraction.

Arnold Thomas noticed that the room felt warmer and vibrated with a different energy – one embracing transition and hope. The Mayor called the people back to the central circle and thanked them for their time. The posted notes were collected to be transcribed and presented to the council. Mayor Mahina encouraged the representatives to email her for a copy of that report and participate in keeping the City Council on task with this project.

The Flamekeeper offered a heartwarming closing benediction. Miles away, the roundhouse glowed, and the earth beneath it shook as if with glee.

Chapter Twenty-Four

Riva was delighted to have Delia visit her and insisted on sending the company plane to get her. The flight from Victoria to Calgary was uneventful in the twin-engine Saab 340D and too quick to require refreshments. Delia nibbled some fruit and sipped champagne. It was nice to be spoiled.

She hadn't heard much from her adoptive father's family since his death. The widow's inheritance had been sufficient for the last years of her mother's life, and Delia remembered that the family had been supportive in their way. They weren't an overly affectionate bunch, as she recalled, so she was surprised when Riva and her three children mobbed her with hugs.

Riva had produced three sons in the last decade. They were handsome young boys and introduced themselves as Amir, who was nine; Malik, who was seven; and Yusuf, who would be five *in three whole days.* Riva patted her belly and advised that *this one better be a girl – there are enough men in this house.*

"Omar is out in the oil fields and won't be back in town until Friday night," said Riva. Amir, Malik and Yusuf were excused from the room to play video games. However, Yusuf clung to Delia's arm and looked up at her with big brown puppy dog eyes. Delia kissed him on the cheek. He responded with a massive grin, running out and calling to his brothers: "*She KISSED me!*" Delia and Riva shared a chuckle.

"Oh, yes. Omar and Nasir run the family's Canadian oil production. So how is that going?" asked Delia, sitting on a soft settee in a huge great room filled with furnishings and elaborate artwork.

"They are doing very well and have many employees in the oil fields. There is also an office here in Calgary that Nasir's sons manage," replied Riva.

"That's right. My father worked there before I came along. And you all live here on this estate?" asked Delia. "Nasir's family and yours together?"

"Nasir, his children and wives live in the larger building over there," said Riva, pointing out the large window west of the room. "Omar, myself and our children live in this building, and there are servants' quarters between us."

"How many children and wives does Nasir have? He must be over eighty years old,' commented Delia, squinting to remember her father's uncle.

"76 years old last month," replied Riva. "He has the two sons and three daughters and only two wives now – several have been ill and passed away."

"Omar never wanted another wife?" asked Delia.

"Wanted, but not going to happen. My uncle and his sons will do as they wish, and if they treat their wives well, I have nothing to say about it. My husband is another matter. I am his wife, and my children our heirs, and that is the only way my father would allow me to marry beneath my station."

"Interesting. Thank you for sharing that, Riva. "

"Now, about you. My mother tells me you were home looking for information about your adoption. I gather you found very little," she said.

Delia told Riva about the DNA test results, the letter from England, and the connection to Riva. The other woman nodded thoughtfully and listened closely.

"What was the missing girl's name?" she asked.

"Jennifer McLean – or Jenny, " replied Delia.

"White women are living in many of Saudi's wealthy family compounds. They are servants in the women's quarters. The women's gossip is that they are concubines who have aged or fallen out of favour for some reason. I often wondered why they would not work elsewhere, but there is a debt owed that can be sold or traded, or so my father told me once," said Riva.

"Do you think Jennifer is still alive somewhere in one of these compounds?" asked Delia.

"I was going to say so, yes, but I just realized that one of my uncle's wives has some visitors right now. Her mother and her mother's servants. I am told two women and a man are in the mother's entourage. One of the women has very fair skin and hair. My maid commented that her hair is spun white and gold sugar. They call her *Jen.* Likely a coincidence, but... "

Delia felt a whirlwind of emotions pass through her body. *Had she found her birth mother? Was this too good to be true? What if she doesn't want to know her daughter? What if it isn't her?*

"What if they won't let her go and it is my mother?" she asked.

"Well, first, let's find out if it is her. Do you have those photographs?" asked Riva. Delia nodded and rummaged in her bag for them.

Riva pushed a buzzer on the wall. "Have Samira come to the great room, please?"

A few moments later, a woman of about 35 wearing black dress pants and a black overblouse with a pattern of tiny yellow flowers entered the room.

"Yes, Ma'am?"

"Do you remember telling me about Kalida's mother's maid?" asked Riva.

"The white hair – Jen? Yes," said Samira.

"Could this be her, but much younger?" asked Riva, passing Samira the photos. Samira looked at each image closely.

"She is much older looking but has the same smile when she watches the young children playing," affirmed Samira.

"Do you know where Jen is now?" asked Riva.

"She's working in the garden with Layla,' replied Samira.

According to Delia's estimation, the garden Riva had ten acres of planted rows and pruned trees. About 100 yards into the garden, amongst the corn stalks, were two bright straw hats. Riva walked into the field with Delia, and as they approached the women, she said:

"Layla? Could you help me find some early tomatoes for dinner?

"Oh, sure. We've got some big juicy ones, Ma'am."

Layla and Riva walked to another area of the garden. Delia smiled at the other woman, who removed her straw hat and wiped her brow with her sleeve. Delia could hear her mother say, *Don't use your sleeve, Delia! That's why we have paper towels.*

"Hi. My name is Delia. Samira says you are called Jen. Is that right?"

"Yes," said Jen, lowering her eyes and becoming agitated.

"Don't worry, Jen. I just wanted to say hello. I heard you had the same hair colour as I do and thought that was cool. Everyone in the family has brown hair and eyes. I used to get teased in the Saudi orphanage because my hair was blonde and my eyes were blue, but my skin was brown. That's why I was adopted by Riva's cousin and his white wife. My birth mom was white; I just discovered her name was Jennifer McLean, and I ..." Delia paused and wiped her nose on her sleeve. "I dunno – I hoped that you were her. I want to find my mom." Then, Delia sat down in the garden earth and sobbed into her elbow.

Silence. Jen sat very still. Layla took a basket of tomatoes into the kitchen. Delia could feel Riva standing behind her. The tears subsided, and she wiped her face. Jen was kneeling close to her; she lifted Delia's face, looked intently at her face, and deep into her eyes.

"When were you born?" whispered Jen.

I don't know for sure. The orphanage decided I was a week old when I was dropped off there. So my ID shows May 6, and I'm 26 years old," whispered Delia.

"April 28th. Oh! I can't believe it. They told me my baby was dead!" cried Jen. "How did you find me?"

Delia told Jen about the DNA test and letters from Mrs. McLean.

"Oh my god!" exclaimed Jen. "My parents searched for me? I was told they didn't want me back."

"Your father has passed away, but your mother is still hoping," said Delia.

"Moira didn't make it," said Jen, fully expecting the confirming head shake. It had been a nightmare, she'd seen many of the girls beaten to death, but she had survived.

Riva coughed. Jen was startled, and her eyes opened wide with terror.

"Did you tell Jen that your DNA is connected to me, too?" she asked.

"What?" Jen's head was whirling. This was all confusing.

"Riva is my adoptive father's first cousin, but the DNA test suggests that she's a more distant cousin," said Delia, and then turning to look at Riva, "You never told me why your DNA was in the RelativeDNA system."

Layla appeared to call Jen into the kitchen to assist with the meals for the other household Jen looked afraid. Delia told her to go on as usual and that they would meet again soon.

Riva and Delia returned to the great room. Riva took out her phone, poked at the screen, and then put the device to her ear.

"Kalida? Would you and your mother like to join us in the east dining room for coffee this evening? We have a guest that I'd like you to meet."

* * *

Delia enjoyed a lively dinner with Riva and her children. Yusuf sat beside Delia and watched her intently, smiling at her whenever she looked his way. Amir sat on the other side of her, steadfastly ignoring her. Malik laughed at them and told her jokes. Riva took all this in and shook her head.

"Such a travesty. Young men so intent on a strange woman in the house and leaving their poor mother to starve without food being passed to her humble self." Riva feigned sorrow but winked at

Delia. "What will your father say about these things happening in his home?"

Delia stifled a giggle with her napkin. The boys passed all of the dishes served to Riva. Amir left his chair to serve food onto her plate and fill her glass. Then he returned to his chair, sticking his tongue out at Malik and poking Yusef as he passed him.

Delia chatted with the boys about their studies. She found that they were more interested in the newest versions of computer games and touring the property on their bikes as a group of galaxy-protecting heroes. Delia told them she would love to interview them for her paper one day and gave them her card each.

After dinner, the boys went off to play, inspired to greatness by this promise of celebrity status. Riva and Delia chatted while the table was cleared and coffee was served.

"Excuse me for one quick moment," said Riva, stepping into the next room. She returned shortly, holding a file folder.

Kahlida and her mother, Zahra, entered the room and seated themselves at the table. Riva's staff served them coffee, and a platter of tiny cakes was served.

"Who is this guest that you command us to attend?" said Zahra, eyeing Delia suspiciously.

"Mother, really, *command?*" said Kahlida. "It was a lovely invitation, Riva. Thank you." She selected a cake and nibbled on it.

"I wanted you to meet my cousin, Delia," said Riva, gesturing to Delia. "She has come to visit us from British Columbia. We have not seen each other since my wedding. Her parents are now gone, and she misses being with her family. "

"She looks to your family's money then? A poor, destitute relative?" commented Zahra, with tight lips and crossed arms.

"No, but I am looking to purchase your property on her behalf because family is important to me, and you have some of her family in your household." Riva opened the file folder before her and chose a document to read.

"What nonsense is this?" I am a poor widow and have no property. I live here in the good graces of my son-in-law." Zahra's demeanour changed completely.

Delia wondered at the amazing transformation and decided that the movie 'Monster-in-law' might have been miscast.

"This is the signed agreement of betrothal for Kahlida to marry Nasir. Nasir's father presented your husband with a mahr of 30,000 riyals and two white servant women, Jennifer and Susanna, valued at 6,000 and 5,000 riyals, respectively. From my understanding, these women have lived in your Saudi home. Is that who accompanies you here?"

"No, Susanna is gone," said Zahra, "I sent her daughter to live here before my husband died. To keep her safe from him."
"She came to me as a teenager. Jen arrived with my mother recently," finished Kahlida.

"Jen is my birth mother," said Delia. "I was adopted from an orphanage in Saudi."

"By my cousin and his wife," added Riva, "so I'd like to reunite the family and purchase Jennifer from you for the original value of 6, 000 riyals."

"Susanna is gone, as in dead or sold? I'd also like to discuss the purchase of Layla because they seem to have a strong friendship." Delia's instincts told her that Susanna was likely trafficked, too.

"Gone and buried at sea," said Zahra. "I was told that she fell from the family yacht and drowned. I suspected she was trying to escape again, but women are not told much."

The women sat silently for a long moment. Then Kahlida said, "I would agree to Jen and Layla simply joining your household as it seems long overdue, but I'm sure Nasir would be pleased with some monetary compensation. Shall we let him and Omar sort it out?" She looked at Zahra, who nodded, looking at her hands.

Riva's brown eyes met Delia's blue ones. They shared a smile and nodded.

"Well, that's it then," said Riva. "More coffee, anyone?"

Chapter Twenty-Five

Peter strolled along the roadway carrying a blue recycling bucket filled with plastic containers and pasteboard packaging. He approached the community recycling bin and lifted the lid of *Cardboard Only.* He set the bucket on the ground and bent to gather his offerings. Jalissa came up the road from the other direction, pulling a small wagon with similar items.

"Getting chilly again. I think summer is about done," said Peter.

"Ya. Some short time this year. De pool always needs fixin', or it be raining," responded Jalissa. Peter was always friendly and told funny stories. He was a nice neighbour. Not like the cranky white bitch two doors down from her with the yappy dog. She was a piece of work, that one.

Items were sorted into respective bins, and both returned to their homes. Peter liked to walk along the water's edge and take photos of sunsets, moon risings and the various birds or wildlife co-habiting in his neighbourhood.

The second anniversary of the Wolf Attack at Meeachan Park had come and gone. Spring had been brief, followed by a summer working event staff at the soccer stadium or the occasional concert at the arena. It wasn't a full-time gig by any stretch, and he'd be glad when hockey season returned in the next few weeks. Unfortunately, retirement was a bit slow, and his old bones complained of inactivity.

Karl's cancer was still in remission, and he'd adopted a dog named Maizey to celebrate his healing. The trio embraced this new little lady, and the family was fulsome for the addition.

Lisa had completed a novel and was enjoying a busy new career in publishing and podcasting. She had an interview later that day with a new client, a journalist writing a memoir. Lisa was meeting her in a downtown cafe and had already walked to the bus stop.

Peter met Karl at the door of their home as the latter returned from walking Maizey. Dog in crate and gear gathered the two men and left for the stadium. A red patterned sash hung over the back of Peter's car seat, and a BC Metis Nation membership decal was displayed proudly on the lower left front windshield.

While driving along their complex's winding driveway, Peter negotiated an inordinate number of speed bumps. Karl grumbled about the bumpy process interrupting his texting.

Several cars passed them entering the complex, and he paused to allow Jalissa to turn out of her townhouse's parking spot and onto the main driveway. Peter and Jalissa exchanged waves, then exited the complex onto a sidestreet, pausing at the next intersection. Jalissa turned right, and Peter turned left, going about their business.

Bembe and Ronica chatted about their school days as Jalissa drove to Cai Hong's home. Tanisha was working at the arena tonight and would not be coming for dinner. Mei Ling and Wei Chan were lovely people and had invited them for a joint family dinner, which Cai Hong and Bembe had requested at least once a month over the years. Jalissa reciprocated as often as her schedule would allow.

Meanwhile, Cai Hong's family gathered around the dining room table, preparing for their guests' arrival. Wei Chan lit the candles while Mei Ling set the plates and silverware. Cai Hong was excitedly bouncing around the room and was eager to welcome his best friend, Bembe.

Pulling into their driveway, Jalissa parked, and Bembe ran ahead, barely waiting for the car to stop. Jalissa and Ronica snickered over his excitement and entered the home with a door standing ajar and no one there. Cai Hong had let Bembe in, and the two had disappeared. Wei Chan greeted them and apologized for his disappearing son. He took their jackets and ushered them into the living room. Mei Ling stuck her head out of the kitchen and greeted them, advising them that dinner would be ready shortly.

These evenings were a long-standing tradition between the two families. They had become even more significant since the traumatic incident at Meeachan Park. *The Day of the Wolves*, as the boys called it, had been overwhelming for Jalissa, who had been at work and unable to attend the field trip, and Mei Ling, who had stepped in to offer her assistance to the teacher. One could not be there to protect her children, and the other had kept the boys safe and watched for Ronica. The stress of that day bonded the two women in appreciation and humility.

Wei Chan called his son and Bembe to the dining room. The two families sat together, and Mei Ling served the food. She had prepared a traditional Chinese meal with dumplings, stir-fried vegetables, and steamed rice. Jalissa enjoyed the cultural exchange and always made the meals at her house with dishes from her Jamaican heritage.

The group chatted about their day as they ate, and the adults shared stories about their childhood experiences. Cai Hong and

Bembe were eager to show Wei Chan their latest gaming levels, so they played together in Cai Hong's room. Ronica helped clear the table, and Jalissa visited with Mei Ling while cleaning the kitchen. After the tasks were done, the women sat at the table and played a board game while drinking tea.

As the night ended and the visitors prepared to leave, Jalissa hugged Mei Ling and expressed her gratitude for the warm and welcoming environment Cai Hong's family had provided. Mei Ling and Wei Chan assured Jalissa that the Williams family was welcome anytime, not just Bembe. Mei Ling said that the friendship between the two families would always be there to support them all through difficult times.

Wei Chan said, "I am grateful for the opportunity to provide comfort and support to our friends."

"There is power in good food and a welcoming environment to provide healing and comfort," said his wife in agreement.

"We could do it every night!" declared Cai Hong

"And when would you do your homework, young man?" asked Jalissa.

"EXACTLY!" exclaimed Cai Hong and Bembe in unison.

Chapter Twenty-Sis

Lisa entered the café and found a seat near the back. The music overhead was mellow and likely wouldn't bother the audio of her recording. However, it was a copyright strike waiting to happen. Blocking it out was probably possible, but she'd leave that to Karl to determine later.

Delia hustled in the door, spotted Lisa and waved. Sitting at Lisa's chosen table, Delia propped her backpack on the adjacent chair and slipped off her jacket.

The waitress took their orders, and then they were left to small talk. Laptops were set up, and Wifi was accessed. The two women discussed processes and agreed on a plan of action. Since Delia had emailed a summary of her memoir project and impressive bio before the meeting, Lisa was prepared to proceed with the interview. First, however, Delia wanted time to review the direction of the questions. Lawyer turned journalist, and now champion of trafficked women made Delia a podcaster's dream, so Lisa was happy to adapt.

"Fair enough, Delia," said Lisa, "I'm also happy to chat off the record and decide together what direction the podcast should take."

"No, it's okay. Go ahead and record. I'm anxious that the message isn't lost, so let's go for it," replied Delia.

"Tell me why that message is so important to you. Tell me about Jennifer," said Lisa as she tapped the *record* button.

The waitress brought muffins and tea. Lisa sipped on her tea and wondered if this adoptee had found wholeness. She remembered a similar file crossing her desk.

"Jennifer is beautiful and loving but very damaged by her life experience. She wakes in the night screaming from PTSD nightmares. It is beyond heartbreaking that someone so gentle and kind would be treated so monstrously."

"I can't imagine the horror of abduction and enslavement," said Lisa, nodding.

Delia related the journey to find her birth mother and the first meeting in Riva's garden.

"Amazing coincidence! That she would be there in your uncle's household," said Lisa.

"No coincidence. Riva knew as soon as I told her RelativeDNA linked us. She had met Jennifer a decade before when my father's youngest uncle, Nasir, married his fourth wife. His father, Bandar, gave my mother to the bride's father as part of a dowry payment along with another trafficked woman. My adopted father's Great Uncle, Bandar, is my birth father. His first wife told my adoptive parents of my existence in the orphanage. She had wanted to keep me under her care, but my obvious mixed breeding mortified Bandar. He wanted me drowned, but she persuaded him to send me to an orphanage and kept in touch with them. Jennifer was banished from his bed and sight but remained in the servants' quarters of their Saudi home until the dowry trade."

Delia paused and sipped her tea, lost in thought. Lisa noted the meekness in her posture and the lost child in her eyes. Not being wanted for whatever reason was a hard pill to swallow. It often got caught in the throat, choking out healing and sabotaging self-worth.

"So what happened next? How did Jennifer come home with you?"

"Well, to Nasir's widowed mother-in-law, Jennifer was a commodity," Delia said with a grimace. "I suppose not many can say they bought their mother, but I can."

Riva had made the initial purchase arrangement, but Delia had paid her every cent back. Riva understood the pride, although she would have accepted the cost as atonement for not doing something sooner.

Jennifer had cried and hugged both Delia and Riva. It took some time to adjust to being free and not having to serve Delia once they were in Victoria. "Jennifer had family members in Canada who were willing to provide her with support and assistance, so we were able to work with Global Affairs to apply for legal status and a temporary residence permit." Delia continued. "This culminated in an award-winning series of articles on the epidemic of human trafficking on a global scale. The best moment was the phone call to Mavis McLean. Three generations of women were wounded to the core by the deeds of unscrupulous persons. Healing tears of joy and declarations of the love that no trauma could erase."

"What a touching story!" said Lisa. "And that is exactly how I'd like to present it on my podcast." *Tap.* "By the way, what happened to the other trafficked woman in the dowry trade? Did you ever find out?"

"Yes. Susanna was also trafficked from a vacation to Romania and was a US citizen. Her daughter, Layla, was purchased by Riva in the same negotiation as Jennifer. Riva was fond of Layla and wanted to help her. She worked with several agencies to establish Susanna's citizenship and connect with her family. Closure came to them with confirmation of Susanna's passing, followed by the celebration of news of a grandchild. Layla remains in Riva's household but visits her extended family in Michigan every Christmas." Delia sipped her Chai Latte thoughtfully.

"Amazing!" said Lisa.

* * *

Tim and Sara Mansfield sat at a table closer to the washroom. Sara was hyper-vigilant about the location of restrooms in any establishment these days. Eight months pregnant with twins, she was tired, excited and not just a little anxious about the next few weeks of her life. Tim was supportive, loving and thoughtful. He had suggested counselling, and the process had been such a reprieve in their marriage. She didn't realize that he had been so distressed by the death of their first child. She had born that pain and sense of failure alone wrapped up in self-loathing. It was an awakening to discover that he had done the same. Sharing the grief and self-doubt had made it easier to trust biology and risk parenthood again. The honeymoon phase returned to their relationship, and he couldn't wait to see her after work every day. She found that endearing and fell in love with him all over again.

"While you make your trip to the ladies' room, I'll grab a box of treats for the office," said Tim, helping Sara to her feet.

"Ohhh, another chocolate chip muffin would be nice for later," said Sara with a smile and batted her lashes. Tim's heart lept and he knew that he would move mountains, climb over a fire, and punch out a lion for her any day of the week.

Tim selected muffins and pastries. It was his turn to buy the meeting goodies for the weekly staff barometer meeting. Julia had brought in an expert on employee engagement and sexual harassment education. It was an embarrassing and painful process at first. He'd considered quitting but understood that he would likely be an ass in the workplace regardless of what workplace, so he stayed and sucked it up. He learned or unlearned a lot and felt he was a better co-worker and husband for the effort.

Chapter Twenty-Seven

The leaves changed colour and fell from the trees as the seasons cycled through the year. The winds of change had whistled through the city, wrapping around the buildings and pulling at the people as they trudged through their routines. Meeachan Park had disputed its manicured status and expressed a need to recover its wild side. Lush undergrowth housed an abundance of animals and birds.

The petting zoo had been repurposed into a training centre for dairy farming, and organic products were produced for area residents and employment for encampment tenants.

The city had built a warming centre on the park's north end, which included a reception area and a satellite medical, mental health, and addictions clinic office. This was staffed in rotation by the Vancouver Island Health Authority and funded by a brilliant collaboration of public and private resources. Unhoused people could drop in to get warm, use the shower, use the laundry facilities and get first aid attention.

A landline phone was available, and a small cafeteria with sandwiches and pop, coffee or tea. Everything was donated and free to the public needing services. There was someone there 24 hours a day to help, refer, and ensure everyone's safety. Stella and her friends volunteered there, in addition to the thrift shop. Stella was often seen consulting with warming centre clients on items they might need from the thrift shop. She had a particular weakness for children and toy purchases.

Near the warming centre, an area once a cricket field had recently provided a first harvest of vegetables to local food banks and encampment residents who worked the garden. James Bay Garden Club volunteers mentored the creation and trained a dedicated group of budding agriculturists. The knowledge that their work fed them and contributed to feeding the community was tremendous for people marginalized by countless issues and an essential part of limiting the community's carbon footprint.

Jacob was the unofficial mayor of Jacob's Place, a city-approved camping area near the totem pole at the park's south end. He greeted and advised all the new homeless encampment tenants and mediated disputes. His wit and wisdom overflowed and embraced all.

The city had built another structure on the north side of Dallas Road near Mile Zero of the TransCanada Highway. This could be used as a warming centre. Still, its primary focus was a food bank and training centre for people to learn job and life skills, have a mailing address, and access Wi-Fi. Joy and Sam worked with learners while Joy's husband, James, managed the food bank and its staff of volunteers. There was a landline phone there, too. It was funded entirely by private donations, one of which ensured that Jacob's pastries were a daily delivery.

On the south side of Dallas Road was a parcel of land that technically belonged to Meeachan Park but had been used as a leach-free dog park for years. The city and the Friends of Meeachan Park opened it up for submissions of designs for inexpensive multi-family housing. It was a lengthy process requiring committees and approvals of several layers of government and legal jousting. The wheels turned slowly and were not without conflict and controversy. However, construction began on three apartment buildings made of recycled materials, including shipping containers and state-of-the-art environmentally sensitive technology. Victoria was raising the bar on social housing and climate change protection!

Officer Ira Goldie volunteers as a bouncer-in-drag at a local club. He is cozy with the wonderful woman who tends the bar and tells him regularly that he is fantastic and loved. Officer Henry Zajic and his wife Stella share their home with Joy, James, and their children. Henry appreciates a second chance at being a good father and has made the most of that opportunity. Stella is supportive and enjoys close friendships with Joy and her family.

The roundhouse was cleansed and updated with as few modifications as possible. The local pagan community, specifically the Ord Brigadeach's local members, held ceremonies within its walls. Brigid, Anu, and the Morrigan may have smiled down on their efforts, blessing them with healing and fertility for the earth around the structure.

As a result, the gardens grew to surplus, the food bank bulged with donations, the animals multiplied, and the people lived safely. Occasionally, a crow would hang about watching the campers, or a lone wolf would prowl through the woods. Either one would disappear behind a tree from whence a woman in white appeared, honouring the legend of the Morrigan. The troublesome Pucas would harass ducks in the north pond, and sometimes, in the still of the night, the scream of a Banshee awakened those who knew the tales, but others would think of owls and go back to sleep.

But the firepit in the roundhouse always burned, and the cauldron bubbled. The hearth was tended, and the healing arts stood at the ready. One could discern prophecies if one looked into the cauldron water as it stilled for scrying. One could see the transitions needed and find the inspiring motivation for that growth.

Translations:

The government workers' conversation:

"*Ahh...regarde! Nous pouvons déplacer ce paragraphe vers le haut et mettre le tableau ici*" French: Oh...look! We can move this paragraph up and put the table here.

"*Oui! Cela fontionnera parfaitement,*" French: Yes! It will work perfectly.

Cai Hong's conversation with his dad:

"*Jù ba, ér zi, wǒmen huí jiā ba*" Chinese Pinyin: Hurry ok, son, we return home, ok

"*Hǎo de, bàba. Wǒ qù ná wǒ de bèibāo.*" Chinese Pinyin: Goodly, father. I go to seize my own knapsack.

Delia's comment on the plane:

"*Shukran jazilan lak, Fatima.*" Arabic: Thank you very much, Fatima.

Jacob and Jalissa's family speak English with heavy accents. Read those bits of dialogue aloud if it is not clear.

Babel fish – a reference from The Hitchhiker's Guide to the Galaxy, by Douglas Adams: "If you stick a Babel fish in your ear, you can instantly understand anything said to you in any form of language."

About the Author

Elle Hawkweed is a Flamekeeper of the Ord Brigadeach, a Third-degree Priestess of the Celtic Pagan Tradition, a Society of Celtic Shamans graduate, and a gifted healer of several modalities, including Therapeutic Touch. Her ability to facilitate healing is well known. The focus of her Shamanic meditations and practices is in tune with her sisters worldwide, who seek to heal the planet and bring comfort to those who suffer.

Elle lives in Victoria, BC and spends a great deal of time communing with the beauty of forest and sea.